NIRVANA DREAMS

Benjamin Joe

Printed in the United States of America

Nirvana Dreams/ Joe: 1st Edition

ISBN: 978-1-7324191-6-2

1.Title 2. Coming of Age 3. Music 4. Nirvana (Band/Music)
5. Drama 6. Joe

Cover Image by © Philip Burke
Please visit *philipburke.com* for more information

NFB
NFB Publishing/Amelia Press
119 Dorchester Road
Buffalo, New York 14213

For more information visit Nfbpublishing.com

Dedicated to

Keri & Tyler

PART I

1.

A boy packs a suitcase under a red glow in his small bedroom. The walls around him are plastered with pictures of Kurt Cobain. Some of them are posters. Others are just grainy newspaper photos.

In the suitcase is one pair of jeans and a few t-shirts. There is an assortment of tapes, a green baseball cap with a Nirvana logo on the back and some socks. He packs without passion, without enthusiasm, without fear, without grief. He is in the eye of the storm that has finally dropped him off here. Somehow, he can hear the blowing of winds against his window, but within the room there is an eerie calm. He knows these winds inevitably will break in and carry him away from here forever. The feedback roars.

In another part of town, a gathering of friends and relatives are mixing on the front lawn of a large manor. The boy's teachers are here. His old karate mentor, his cousins who live in Seattle. His black sheep uncle who no one has heard from in years is here, too, with his girlfriend and her son. Over them is a big banner proclaiming the date and the reason for this assembly.

"HAPPY 17ᵗʰ BIRTHDAY!!" In big, spray painted capital letters the words shine in the light of the afternoon sun. Everyone is happily awaiting the object of their celebration. They're drinking punch and chatting around the big in-ground pool, now covered in this warm November. It had snowed about a week before, but since then it had melted like it never came and people pretended it was still summer.

Back in his room across town the boy finishes his packing. He is of average weight and height. Long straight, brown hair that rests on his shoulders. He has blue eyes and dark eyebrows over a hawk nose and pink lips. His clothes are in the current fashion; baggy jeans, ripped at the knees and cuffed. He's wearing a Bleach T-shirt and around his pale, scrawny neck is a pair of headphones that strings down to his pocket.

He picks up his suitcase. It's a white rectangle bag that looks like it just came out of a department store and is covered in stickers from local bands. For a moment, he stands in the doorway, staring back at his room; his home of laughter, tears and loneliness. The winds pick up, the final chords ring out as he turns his back and fades from view of the doorway.

A few hours later the sun has begun to fall quickly over the party and the people's smiles have been replaced with pensive expressions. There is something wrong, that is for sure, but no one knows quite what. The authorities have been called, but the boy is not in jail or the hospital. His mother is sitting in a lawn chair, staring down the street he is expected to come from. No one appears. In the corner, his friends look at each other in disbelief, not sure whether to be grieving, happy, or just bitter?

The rest of the party is dying down. The punch bowl is emptied while uncomfortable people make their goodbyes and drive home wondering in a vague, worrisome way wondering what had happened and what was to come. Soon the only people remaining are the immediate family.

A little girl about eleven years old is pulling on the pant legs of any adult in the vicinity. She looks up with creased eyebrows and asks where her brother is. No one gives her an answer except for some assurances that everything is just fine. Her father is on the phone, calling anyone he can think of. The boy's mother sits in the living room while her parents comfort her and her mood steadily spirals into hysteria. The uncle stands outside with a smoke.

But the boy isn't thinking of any of this at all. He is standing on the side of a highway feeling the rush of wind coming off the passing trucks. He stares directly into their tail-lights. In front of him is a pile of papers held down by a rock.

They're all various forms of ID. His learning permit, his birth certificate, social security card, a school ID, a blockbuster renter's card, various letters addressed to him, award certificates and one school photo. On each of them is the name Robert Thompson.

A stream of lighter fluid squirts over the pile. Without hesitation the boy that was Bob Thompson lights a match and watches his life go up in a few puffs of black smoke. The flame grows higher, but the boy turns and walks away. With his suitcase in one hand and the other holding his thumb in the air, he walks out of this life and into the next.

*   *   *

The boy finds himself wandering through an unfamiliar

house with white walls and carpeted floors covered with debris. In his ears is the periodic strumming of a guitar playing the familiar songs of his favorite band, Nirvana.

He follows the music to its source. A long-haired man in his twenties sits in a corner on the floor holding a left-handed acoustic guitar. The figure looks up at the boy. He is immediately recognizable as Kurt Cobain, the surly frontman of the band. He's dressed in a white T-shirt and ripped jeans that he wears like a uniform.

When he sees the boy he stops playing, but the music continues. Kurt smiles up at him. The boy who was Bob smiles back, hesitating and then lifts his hand in a small gesture. Kurt's smile deepens as he reaches out his own, grasping the boy's in a gentle handshake.

For a moment, the boy feels a wave of contentment and peace sweep over him. He finds himself feeling completely at home in this strange, lost place.

Clean and bright colors appear, swirling on the wall over Kurt's head, contrasting with the piles of disorganized clothes, papers and junk that litters the floor. He looks directly into Kurt's eyes that look more and more like Jesus'.

*   *   *

"So, where are you heading?"

The voice isn't Kurt's, it's that of the large trucker who had picked up the boy earlier. His question breaks the boy's sleep and he sits up in a daze, pushing his headphones from his ears and stretching his legs. It takes him a few moments to comprehend the question.

"What?"

The trucker repeats himself while the boy fishes for a cigarette, a Marlboro, from his pocket and lights it. After a long indulgent drag, he answers the trucker's question.

"California," he says, trying to appear worldly. "To L.A."

He takes a few more rapid drags until the cigarette is a little more than a stub. He throws it out the window and watches the splash of light in the side mirror. The trucker takes in his answer thoughtfully and replies in a nonchalant sigh of confirmation.

The conversation clearly doesn't interest him, but this trucker needs something to distract himself from his own exhaustion. He has deep, brown eyes under a protruding forehead and a layer of spiny hairs covering his face. He wears an undershirt, a flannel and a blue cap that covers greasy, black ringlets of hair.

"Goin' to be a movie star are ya?" he says.

The boy doesn't say anything. He just stares out the window at the darkened fields that line the highway. Mindlessly he lights another cigarette, but this time puffs on it slowly, taking his time to form smoke rings in the air. The trucker, not bothered with his lack of response, picks up the conversation without a hint of discomfort.

"My sister was in the show biz, y'know."

"Oh really?" says the boy, more out of habit than anything else. His attention is mostly focused on the rings of his cigarette smoke.

"Oh yeah," continues the trucker. The words roll out of him

like a rehearsed script. While his voice never wavers, his eyes and lips seem troubled. A little bit tense as they survey the road.

"Some Hollywood agent picked her out of a local bar she was working at," he shrugs when he comes to this. "She made a few videos, never really took off. She came back and became a hairdresser."

For a long time, there is silence. Eventually the ride comes to an end and the boy thanks the driver, jumps out the door with his white suitcase and shuts the door with bang. The trucker nods and looks back at the road. He drives off with the same tenseness in his eyes. His lips move silently as the engines roar and he's gone. The boy lights another cigarette and makes his way towards the rickety motel behind the road.

2.

The lobby of the motel is little more than a cement closet painted blue with a worn plastic counter on one end and a few chairs arranged sloppily around a short table on the other. Behind the counter is an aging man with a sunken in face and big, black framed glasses. He is wearing a blue tie on a stained shirt. He looks up at the boy with an evil scowl but says nothing.

"Um… I need a room."

"Eh… single or double?"

"Single."

"Smoking or non?"

"Smoking."

"You got an ID?"

"Yeah."

The boy hands him a piece of plastic with his face on it. It proclaims him to be Tommy Cocay, 18. The old man studies it without much scrutiny and hands it back.

"That'll be seventy dollars."

"That much?"

"That's right, take it or leave it."

Reluctantly Tommy hands over three twenties and a ten, a sum that drastically lowers his funds. A little bit worried, he counts the rest as he picks up the key.

"So, where can I get something to eat around here?" he asks without looking up.

"Right through the door," says the older man, also not looking up.

Tommy nods to himself and walks over the left wall where there's a door that proclaims "LOUNGE" in neon letters above it.

The lounge is another disappointment. A bar masquerading as a family restaurant, but the water stains in the ceiling's corners give it away. An unfriendly-looking waitress with dark, red lipstick smeared on her lips, deep wrinkles around her nose and a puckered mouth that gives her face the appearance of an overripe plum is washing the front counter that clearly used to be the bar's only occupied surface.

Most of the chairs are damaged in one way or another. Cigarette burns, duct-taped cuts and holes, splintered wood along the sides, scuff marks and chewing gum. The lights are halogen bulbs set inside glass shades that, when peered through, give the appearance of two shining lights instead of one. Very few people are sitting here. Most of them are still at the bar.

There is an old drunk, no other word for him. Maybe he's a trucker, a construction worker, maybe the manager on his off-shift. He's wearing a black vest and there's this cap, a big, cheap visored-hat. Plastic screen in the back and foam in the front, all sitting beside his drink. Its tip points towards the man's forearm which is big and covered with black hair. He's only semi-conscious, his eyes straight ahead... he's a staring corpse.

He's a couple seats away from the glowering waitress and

occasionally his lips open. A guttural sound emerges. The waitress fetches this and that. On his left, by the far-side of the room, next to a dirty window which is partially blocked by a notice of rates and specials, sits a young mother and two children. By the payphone and the cigarette machine is a middle-aged man speaking rapidly into the payphone's receiver.

The man slips a hand through his hair then puts it on his hip. For clothes he has on a brown, possibly imitation, leather jacket, really blue jeans, a belt and cheap boots like you get out of a catalog. He looks pretty clean, fit really, but in that overly stable ate-every-day sense, maybe had a gym membership. His whole family looks that way, but the kids are on their way to just chubby. His wife, or girlfriend, is a small thing with thin fingers and eyes like a sparrow, darting here and there. She whispers commands and admonishments to her children.

Tommy walks into this scene still thinking about cash. Expenses. Sacrifice. He goes right to the bar but doesn't sit down. Instead he leans against the counter. He combs the overhanging menu for the best deal with his eyes. While he's doing this, he takes in drag after drag of his cigarette. Half gone, his mouth waits for something else to do. Eventually he decides on a grilled sandwich, fries and water. It seems the best thing for both of his organs. Just 2.18 with tax.

By this time his cigarette is gone and he stubs it into the ashtray. Then he digs for the pack that he assumes holds another one. He was wrong. None left. He winces with slight annoyance. That's another three dollars to waste, he thinks. The waitress steps over to him and he quietly tells her his order which she writes down with a stubby pencil and a dirty look. Once she leaves, he crosses the room to the cigarette machine.

While he's shoving in quarters, a couple walk up, a black man and asian girl about Tommy's age. They take the place of the family who have left to their room. The man isn't tall, but he's large in a way that can't be pinned down. Sturdy, stout and solid. He has a neutral expression and short, very cropped, curly hair.

The girl is smaller. Very young, Tommy thinks. About seventeen. She's got long straight hair, brown eyes and is dressed in clean stockings and a black low-cut dress. Tommy watches her as she lights her cigarette, a menthol by the look of the packaging. Her fingernails are painted red and her face is made-up well with eyeshadow and lipstick.

The man walks to the bathroom and the girl is left standing with one leg crooked, idly looking over Tommy's head reading the pay phone signs. She smokes carefully, making sure not to stain the filter with her lipstick. Her other hand plays with her bag. Behind her is a white wall with chipped paint and a bulletin board that has tattered copies of Bible Group Schedules stapled to it. On impulse, Tommy walks over.

"Hey…" He smiles until she looks towards him, her eyebrows scrunched into curious fashion.

"Do you got a match?"

He packs the cigarette box against his leg while he asks this, still smiling, even smirking. He feels a sudden rush of power, a sense of being in control that he's felt before, but nowhere as intensely as he feels now. She silently hands over the lighter, watches him spark it and take its first drag. As he hands it back to her she says, "Marlboros?"

Tommy smiles, nods and then smiles some more. For a moment, she looks away like she's considering something. She looks back with the same puzzled, or curious, look on her face.

At this moment, the door to the men's bathroom opens up and her boyfriend trots back out, rubbing his face and softly snorting. The girl walks towards him, the backs of her legs contorting under her dress.

As they pass each other the girl draws in close and takes something out of his hand while kissing his cheek. The man continues to stare straight ahead without focusing on anything.

Tommy observes all of this silently. The rest of the barroom seems oblivious to them. He occasionally looks towards the floor, then up again, puffing on his new cigarette, then back to the floor again. The girl struts into the ladies' room. The man keeps walking to take the space at Tommy's left side.

The man seems to be thinking something over. He walks over to the billboard to inspect the notices there, then turns around and walks back. Tommy keeps smoking until the cigarette burns down to the filter. He takes out another one.

"Hey," says the man, his eyes flickering over to Tommy's hand. "Do you got another of those smokes, by any chance?"

"Yeah… is Marlboro alright?" The man frowns slightly but shakes his head.

"It doesn't matter… what's your name brother?"

Tommy hands over the cigarette.

"Tommy."

"Yeah? Well, my name's Ryan. The girl I was with, that young Jap, her name's Julia." Nodding absently, Tommy looks over to the side of Ryan. He never quite meets the older man's gaze. Ryan takes the time to remove a lighter from his jacket pocket.

"So, Tommy, you here by yourself?"

"Yeah, I got a room for the night."

"Yeah, yeah," Ryan nods to himself. "That's cool man, maybe we can help each other out?"

"How's that?"

"Well, my girl and I have been driving for a few days now and she's really tired of sleeping in the car, y'know? She gets all bitchy and shit. Well, we got to this dump, but the price is fuckin' astounding, y'know. So, we're looking for someone who wants to share, or would be willing to share a room for the night."

"I'm not sure, man." By this time, any amount of power that Tommy felt he had is gone, vanished away and replaced by a fearful apprehension.

"Of course, I'd make it worth your while..."

Magic words. Tommy looks up, interested.

"I don't have much money but I might have something else you'd like. Why don't you come outside with me and we'll talk it out?" Ryan gestures over to the back door. "It's not really something I can take out inside, y'know? Even bathrooms are iffy."

Tommy nods with uncertainty then looks around, weighing the risks. Ryan is already walking towards the door. Confused and uncertain, Tommy steps forward to follow him outside.

Tommy's heart is beating at a thousand ticks per second. Ryan seems calm enough, but Tommy can only see his back which is hunched as he digs into his pockets.

"This will definitely be worth your while, man, believe me. You'll thank me." Tommy grits his teeth and keeps following.

The back of the motel is dark and dirty except for one bug-filled street lamp overhead and that doesn't really give much light. Tommy is acutely aware that the walls are too thick for any sound to pierce. If any violence occurred, there wouldn't be much he could do. Over his shoulder, Tommy can see the pink, neon letters of the motel sign and occasional car headlights whipping by.

They reach a green dumpster and that's when Ryan turns around. Tommy gasps involuntarily. For a split second his thoughts go to a gun or knife, but the only thing Ryan's holding is a plastic bag full of strips of paper.

"This man, is some high-grade acid. I know it's not as good as cash, but you can sell it pretty easily."

"How many hits is it?" Tommy mumbles, just going through the motions. His stomach flipping from being scared to excited. Frightened to eager.

"50, five ten strips, they're worth like five hundred dollars, more depending how much you sell them for. You'll never get a deal like this again, man. All I'm asking for is a quiet place to sleep and take a shower, y'know? So, is it a deal?" Tommy nods once. He knows what the value of drugs are. He's taken and sold quite a few in the last year, but he's never seen so much before.

He supposes that half of the sheet is fake, but even so, it's a lot more there than this young boy has picked up on his radar before. Maybe the West Coast manufactures more of it, he thinks, maybe Ryan is a chemist… maybe it's all fake, not just half of it. The possibilities add up, but drugs… They have a funny way of making themselves known. Besides, tonight they aren't costing a thing, thinks the boy.

Later, roughly five minutes after Ryan shows off the design imprinted over the entire half-sheet, Tommy sticks out his tongue and looks into the mirror as he places one ten-strip delicately into his mouth. He looks at the paper already dissolving on his tongue and smiles.

At the next sink, Ryan is bent over and by this time Tommy isn't scared of him anymore. He's neither afraid of harm or theft. In fact, now fears and what ifs are just another situation far back in the past. In this present there is only the cold certainty that he'd taken the drugs and soon he is going to feel very strange.

Live in the moment, the eternal movement of chemicals flowing around cells into capillaries down into arteries in his chest and brain. Ryan stands up quickly, rubbing his nose. Tommy smiles an idiot grin before they both walk out of the bathroom.

The hallway smells of mint, but it's just Ryan chewing on a piece of gum. Tommy takes one look at the dining room and reaches for another nicotine fix. Ryan is doing the same thing. This doesn't bother Tommy. For just one cigarette, he'd bought a world of dreams. Of high scale living. While all the squares diddle each other, he is living! He is …

"So, like, where is this room, man?" asks Ryan, sweating visibly and looking around with sketched out eyes. He doesn't seem at home.

"Oh, oh yeah," Tommy wretches his eyes off the end of his burning cigarette. "It's room number 244, second floor. Hey, I'll be there in a minute… I gotta pick up my dinner."

"Alright man, we'll see you there." So, they both walk out of the hallway, Ryan heading for the front desk, while Tommy turns over to the bar. He's testing out the drug, looking quickly towards the neon signs in the windows of the bar then to the ground. On a whim, he picks his headphones from around his neck, snaps them over his ears and presses play. Not too loud. He can still hear his surroundings, but his mind zeros in on the recorded radio show of Kurt Cobain's solo performance of "Opinions."

On the bar is his grill cheese sandwich and fries. Moving quickly, he sweeps the plate off the counter and turns around to leave the lounge entirely. The plate is hot, but not hot enough to burn him. The food smells fantastic. Tommy breathes deeply of the unreal aroma.

"Where are you going?"

It's the old waitress, but her voice is far off and Tommy doesn't give it another thought until she steps right in front of him. With her apron swaying and a striped, blue and white towel held like a whip in her right hand, Tommy almost laughs but stops short. She's covered in trails. Every pigment on her face is stretched out across her blouse and the white walls behind her. It's then that Tommy realizes that the drug is working.

"Um… to my room… ma'am," Tommy stutters. He looks wildly from the floor to the ceiling, anywhere to avoid the waitress's gaze, but nothing is helping. The green benches are now slowly rolling and the lamps overhead seem to be throwing graffiti onto the table-tops beneath them. Over it all is a wave of panic that threatens to devour his sight and fragment his reason. In the background, Kurt Cobain talks to the interviewer, completely incomprehensible at this point. The waitress continues to stand there.

"Well, you'll want a box for that. You can't take the plate."

She seems to think this is obvious, as though the very idea is outrageous. She takes the plate out of his shaking hand and before he can even move, replaces it with a box. Tommy stares at her then the box, then the door right in front of him.

"Thank you," he says and he's never meant those words more than now. The door is dark and threatening, but he can feel the stares of everyone in the room on him, so, he screws up his courage, closes his eyes and walks through.

3.

Julia and Ryan are waiting in front of the room, leaning on the balcony and staring up at Tommy as he stumbles on the stairs going up to them.

"You alright?" asks Ryan. Tommy mumbles something in reply while he rips the key out of his pocket and jams it into the door handle. The moon is half-full and nearly set while a cold wind whips around Tommy's fingers. The door jerks open.

The room is small. It sits among a dozen rooms just like it and they're connected by an outdoor concrete walkway. There's a metal banister on the side of this to discourage any accidents. It smells like a cross of smoke, soap and has clean sheets and vacuumed floors. The television is bolted to a wooden bureau that in turn is bolted to the wall. The headboard of the bed is cracked and the corners have little dust balls that were overlooked by the maids. As he enters, Tommy flips the light switch and immediately the dull floral wallpaper begins to move and shift in some melodic dance. The music is at this point loud and noisy, going through the progression of sounds Nirvana experimented with before making Nevermind.

Ryan and Julia follow him, putting down their bags while Tommy falls onto the bed with his suitcase. He stares at the ceiling. Everything is different now. All sense of distance is lost.

Things that seem close are actually quite far away and visa-versa. Try as he might he can't seem to focus on any one object. Ryan says something indistinct. Like buzzing. He takes off his headset and hits the stop button.

"What?" says Tommy and the word then echoes in his head like a mantra. What what what what. Momentarily, he fixes his eyes on Ryan who then proceeds to morph and twist horribly under his gaze.

"I said," Ryan repeats. "Me and Julia will take the floor, we have sleeping bags."

"Sounds good," Tommy says weakly. He tries to put the words in some sort of context. "Sounds good." Ryan nods, or seems to nod. His face is so vastly distorted. On a chair across from the bed, Julia stretches her legs.

"Right, we really appreciate this man." Ryan's voice floats over the room, but Tommy isn't paying attention. He's staring at Julia who appears even more sensual than before.

A glow of trails surrounds her body, especially her lips and hands. He watches, fascinated, as she removes her high heels and takes a moment to rub her feet. Ryan notices this and almost says something, but thinks better of it and walks to the bathroom instead. Tommy doesn't even hear the door close.

In his mind, a halo of white light is surrounding Julia's body with trails of purple and green mixing around in the wallpaper behind her. The sight makes his eyes bulge and his lips draw apart in an 'O' of appreciation.

Then she's looking right at him, the hint of a smile playing across her lips. His breathing halts as their eyes lock across the mere feet that separate them. His pupils inflate with her image. His body is tense with unknown fears and urgings as Julia rises up gracefully, loose and open in the night.

She seems larger than life, easily turning the rest of the room to a mere background. Looking down, she smiles at Tommy's bewildered face and turns to walk to the bathroom, still twisting her head to gently watch and smile in his direction. Tommy stares after her, the drug beating harder and louder, more insistent. The door to the bathroom clicks closed.

Julia leans over the sink while Ryan strokes her hips. His face is set in a twitching neutrality. It would be impossible to know where he came from, though plenty have made guesses. He might be from the ghetto. The projects. Another angry man with desen-sitized morals and a flat, black and white outlook, they think.

Could say he's been abused, though how will never be known. Could've been personal, but could just be a sort of general abuse inherited through his senses while the harsh wind blows over the neighborhood. No one is happy and happy is broken down to sexual domination and monetary wealth. In any case, all those questions, hopes, dreams and fantasies of boyhood are long gone and he is a man. Making it through the world a day at a time. Without thinking. Without questioning. Just another bouncing ball in the pinball machine of the planet.

Julia is younger and as she snorts up the powder on the sink there is a moment of confusion. Don't know where she came from, or how she met Ryan, whether she loves him, or needs him, or is controlled by him. Her dreams are wrapped in a time when she will be secure. When beauty is no longer necessary. When she can sit in her house with blue shutters and talk over the phone. Actually, her dreams are quite vague and she rarely, consciously, thinks about them.

She met Ryan earlier, how much earlier is hard to say, but on that day, she knew they were connected. Here was a real man. A man who would take care of her. Shelter her. Protect her. He'd done all of that.

She'd followed him wherever he went. Helping him. Listening to him and true they'd taken some risks, but what was life if not a risk? You have to take what you want. What you need.

They're a classic couple. An item. A team. A predatory outfit. A defensive unit. They're connected by so many strings that at times when one moves their hand, the other takes a step. It is clear that they share something that is incommunicatable. Just simple touches, maybe a whispered word between each other is all that's needed. They know what to do, thinks all those people. They know how to survive.

Tommy isn't aware of any of this. He's staring at the ceiling. Thinking of silly fantasies. Internal voices contradicting each other every moment. Ryan leans down and whispers something into Julia's ear. She smiles and stands to kiss him. The room spins.

Tommy opens his eyes with a start. Ryan is standing by the bathroom door, saying something.

"I'm going to pick up some ice, alright?"

"Alright," says Tommy, somewhat weakly. Shaking his head.

Trying to get some focus. Ryan smiles and gives a little wave before opening the door. Tommy watches fascinated as Ryan steps into an endless void on the other side and vanishes. The door swings shut just as the bathroom door opens.

Julia emerges. She pauses to lean against the doorframe, her eyes locked on Tommy, who stares back. All sorts of insane and inappropriate thoughts revolving in his brain. She approaches. Her lips are newly colored and she purses then opens them systematically while she walks. Swinging her hips. Now she's standing right in front of the bed. She licks her lips and takes a breath. Tommy says nothing. She seems like she wants to say something. Something to explain or apologize for. Anything to break the silence. Instead she pulls her dress over her head.

Tommy blinks, not quite believing, trying to discern from the fantasies in his head from the reality of the room. He blinks and she's on her knees in front of him, pulling at his pants, staring into his eyes. Her lips move but nothing comes out. The drugs are screaming in Tommy's eyes. Fear and lust are mixing into a fever tone of hard feedback. Every nerve in his body is overloading to the sensation. His eyes are closed. Clenched teeth.

His muscles tense and unleash in a way that's almost painful at a rapid pace and just then the door opens to reveal an outraged Ryan. His mouth open-wide. Teeth gnashing, but no sound. Tommy still lying with closed eyes on the bed... only he's not on the bed, he realizes. He's on the floor, spread-eagled and making gurgling noises. Julia stands up and then rushes to a seat wearing a terse expression. She casually crosses her legs but makes no move to cover her bare chest. Or does she have a bare chest?

The simulation of what has just happened buries itself into Tommy's subconscious and stays there, unable to be recalled by the frontal lobe. Julia's face. She's suddenly looking very predatory. A smile is on her lips and her hair isn't even a little mussed. What. The word echoes again and again.

Ryan pulls the stupefied Tommy off the floor while he struggles to pull his pants back on. Which are on. Which doesn't make sense, because… But it's too late. Shouting, Ryan hurls him out the door while putting his hand into Tommy's pocket and ripping loose bills and the bag of drugs. Tommy stares at him in confusion. The wallet in his back pocket remains intact. The drug still swims in his veins.

*   *   *

Daylight. The sun is coming up from behind the mountains and the trees. There's a layer of dew on the grass and leaves. Tommy is walking down a road. It's one of those small streets that tend to run parallel to the major freeways. The hallucinations are getting steadily smaller and slower and less overwhelming throughout the night, but his brain is a long way from normal.

There's something that happens after tripping hard. For several days, nothing really seems right and by the time it's over things just aren't quite the way they were before. If red lights always gave out those beams, or if the blades of grass always looked so distinct on someone's lawn…

Well, whatever.

Right now, Tommy can feel the cool breeze run down the

road and way up above him, the clouds are moving for reasons only they know. The air is cold and wet. The bottoms of his jeans are soaked. Far more ragged than he'd fashionably intended them to be. The rim on his cap is torn. He doesn't know how it got to be like that.

He doesn't know what his face looks like, but it feels horrible. His cheekbones seem to be sticking out more than they used to. His eyes are just painful slits that the world and all its misery are able to come in through.

Sad, sad, tired day.

He tries to huddle in his sweatshirt, but it's stopped giving warmth a long time ago. The only thing that gives him comfort is walking. One foot in front of the other. Over and over again. Repetitively staying off the madness and keeping him moving.

For some reason, he decided it was very important to move that night. He'd been lucky. No one had pulled over to give him a ride. No cops had decided to fuck with this boy with bad breath and no conversation skills. Luck had been with him.

But where is he going?

West. L.A.

Certainly not home, that was out of the question though he couldn't say why. Dreamily, he thinks about good days when he was small and he used to sled down the big hill on the outskirts of town with his mother and friends. He always seemed to have a lot of friends when he was small.

Anyway, in those days the snow wasn't as cold as it is now. It didn't make grades suffer. It didn't make him antagonize girlfriends. It didn't bring on suicidal thoughts. In those days snow stayed where it belonged. Outside for snowmen and snow forts, sledding and skiing and the occasional friendly fight. If it did come inside it was quickly melted and licked up by the family dog. It didn't linger and it didn't freeze the hearts of everyone inside. In his drug-enhanced, stunted mind, the connection between snow and every personal disaster for the last five years had become firmly intertwined and connected.

These are the way his thoughts go as he walks, slowly to be sure and without his thumb in the air. His suitcase is gone, destroyed in the strange events of the night before. Tommy doesn't even try to remember. What bits came in were too strange to be taken seriously.

The mind of a tripped-out boy is too weird to describe. Even weirder than a normal boy's mind. They tend to hold onto symbols. Father sky, Mother Earth. Bad lights. Good lights. That kind of thing. You can't talk to a person like this. Not without putting them into a panic and certainly not in any normal way. Most people just give up. Wave their hands in the stricken victims' faces and make goofy expressions.

"You see any trails?" they ask, laughing at the poor kid's eyes. "Man, you're really tripped out!"

It's about nine o'clock am when he finally comes out of it. The sun is shining on the right side of his head, stinging his eyes and there's a crosswind that blows into his back. Tommy stops and looks around. The place is deserted, just a strip of road and new trees.

He grunts and half-jumps, half-falls down off the road to the outskirts of the trees. The trees seem to go on forever, but they really only extend about a quarter of a mile before another highway cuts it off. All of these trees have been living on a steady supply of car exhaust since the day they were planted.

The only birds in the sky are black crows that make piercing cries over his head. Tommy unzips his jeans and starts to urinate. He looks up over to a tree branch to watch a squirrel spiral his way up. He stays completely silent, listening to the rush of traffic on the road and the leaves rustling in the wind.

The first pangs of homesickness hit him there, pissing on the side of the road.

4.

He remembers his mother. His father. His girlfriend, Gina. He misses his posse of friends who were all idiots, but they were his idiots and all that he knows. He even misses his room, a place he'd been trapped in many times. Most of all, he misses Gina. She is a conventional chick. She always made it clear that she was rebelling now, but that someday she'd be in college and on her way to being rich. It disgusted him, but that wasn't all of her.

She was a pale, white girl, not frail or petite, but not overweight. She had curly, long, brown hair and brown eyes that were surrounded by mascara. Not a lot, just enough to bring out her face. She always dressed to please, but she wasn't some simpering girl. She had bought into feminism a long time ago and no man was going to stop her. That's why he left eventually, just seeing her confidence, her knowledge that they wouldn't last forever and not even seem bothered. It had been the last straw.

He recalls one particular incident. It had been late August just before school was about to open. They drove in her car, an old 81 Oldsmobile Cutlass, a big boat of a car with bad suspension and worse radio reception, but a perfect backseat. Listening to Alice in Chain's newest album and passing a joint, Tommy began to philosophize on what was before him.

"I don't know, it just seems like things are gonna change and in a big way, y'know? I plan to be right there, right where the action is, maybe be a famous artist or in a band, y'know?" Gina just smiled and nodded as she took a hit, pulled into a back road and then into an inlet beside the beach. It was about midnight now and no one else was on the water. The moon was huge that night. Big, yellow and full with small clouds crossing its perimeter.

They looked at each other in the cool dark, watching the smoke curl and waft in the fishbowled car. Tommy takes another hit.

"I really think I'm like destined for somethin', y'know? You and me both."

Gina bowed her head ever so slightly. Her face was somewhat tan from the summer sun and her hair had some bleach in it. She carefully took the joint Tommy was holding and looked at it.

"Y'know, my parents have been getting on my back about college lately."

"Yeah?" said Tommy. He didn't know what else to say.

"What about yours?"

"Oh, y'know, they go on. I'm not worried. There's more to life than just college."

"Yeah." She took another hit and burned her thumb. She held it away from her chest and coughed. "I think we should put this in a bowl."

Tommy grabbed a bowl out of the glove box and took the roach from her. He ripped the resin soaked paper and put the remaining weed into the glass pipe.

"So?" he asked.

"So, what?" Gina looked confused, but he could see in her eyes that she knew exactly what he was asking.

"So, are you going? To college I mean?" Tommy asked the question quickly, not really wanting to hear the already obvious answer.

"Oh. Well, yeah. Me and my mom have been looking them over, y'know for location and what I want to do…" Tommy lit up the bowl and took a big hit while Gina trailed off.

"So…"

"So."

"This'll be our last year together."

"Why do you say that?" Gina actually looked distressed. Tommy continued looking down.

"Well, I don't want to go to college."

"Bob," she said the name in a small whine. In the present, Tommy remembers how she used to say his former name, and smiles. Not real anymore, but the memory still lingers.

"'Cause I don't want to buy into that! I want to travel and do stuff, not be stuck in a place for four years for what? Stupid parties? Boring professors? Fuck that."

Gina kept her eyes averted on the steering wheel and grabbed the pipe without looking up. Tommy stared at the windshield, making out a cat running across the street.

"Well, Bob, y'know how important college is."

Tommy snorted.

"No, really! It might seem dumb," tried Gina again. "Well, it's not like you can't go. You're smart, you've got money."

"Whatever," Tommy cut the conversation short. "I'll think about it OK?" And then before the mood could be completely broken, he leaned in to give her a kiss.

She was unresponsive at first, slightly hurt. Her eyes looked bloodshot and teary, but eventually she came around. The rest of the night, they listened to the tape, kissed and didn't return to the subject at all.

*   *   *

He picks up a ride soon after returning to the road. A black Chevrolet Wagoneer pulls up beside him. Tommy doesn't even have his thumb out.

The car's beat. Dust has been kicked up all over the hood and sides. It's covered in little dents and flaked off paint.

The driver looks even more beat.

He's a golden-haired Nordic type, but he's really more like a walking dirtball. His hair sticks together in clumps. It's obviously not an intentional dread job, just the natural state of weeks-long-unwashed hair. His nose is clearly defined from the rest of his face. It's skinny with small nostrils and an arrow-like tip. His eyes are hazel green with flecks of gold around the pupils. He's wearing a denim shirt; it sits opened on his chest with nothing underneath. For pants he has a pair of corduroys, originally brown, but now streaked with brightly colored patches.

He looks strong.

His forearms bulge where the sleeves have been rolled up and he sits like a horseshoe. Bent over, but strong as steel.

"You need a ride?" he shouts out of the window, gesturing with his left hand. Tommy nods weakly and stumbles to the car door.

"Where are you headin'?" asks the driver.

Tommy says he's going west and then stands silent for a second before offering his name. The syllables feel unnatural. He has yet to assume his new identity. The driver rolls his eyes and opens the door. It opens a crack, but he suddenly pulls it back. For a moment Tommy thinks it's all a cruel joke.

"You look beat, man. Get in the back and lay down, I'm goin' to Texas. That far enough for you?" Tommy smiles and nods while he opens the back door. The seat is covered with a good amount of trash, but also a couple of blankets and some padding. He wipes off the trash and drags himself into the car. As the door closes, the driver guns the engine and they're off down the road.

"Name's Dan," says the driver extending his hand over his shoulder. Tommy grabs it with a weak grip before letting go.

"Good to meet you…" Tommy grunts.

"Great, Tommy, you just go to sleep now. Don't worry. I haven't killed anyone yet and I don't intend to now. We'll talk later." Tommy doesn't say another word. He shuts his eyes and almost immediately falls asleep.

*   *   *

He finds himself standing backstage. The air is hot. Dozens of sweaty people push their way by him carrying boxes, instruments, amplifiers, ladders. Onstage he can see the band finishing up their last set. He applauds along with everyone else as the last chord rings out in a fury of feedback and screams.

The band retreats quickly, leaving their broken instruments on the stage for someone else to clean up. Tommy cries 'congratulations' as they pass. Kris and Dave smile at him. They're tired, hot, but still friendly. Kurt just walks by, hunched over, staring ahead towards his dressing room. Tommy looks over to Kris for an explanation, but he just shrugs.

Outside the fans are milling around, some of them are still screaming for another encore, but most are filing out in an orderly fashion. Orderly as in they are jumping up and down and knocking over the people in front of them. Everyone communicates at a shout. Anything lower would be lost in the din. The collective ear drum damage in the crowd could be enough to fill several hundred cabinets of medical files and give jobs to a million hearing-aid factory assemblers.

Tommy stares after Kurt, watching until he slams the door to his dressing room. Even over the din you can hear the pounding. Kris and Dave are moving with the rest of the crew, making no moves to see how Kurt feels. Tommy feels confused.

Then Tommy is in the room with Kurt. He's behind him, watching his face in the mirror. Eyes are closed, shoulders shaking. There's a tension inside him that Tommy can't understand. It feels like a time bomb that's just waiting to be unleashed. Ever so tentatively, a little scared, Tommy puts out his hand and places it on Kurt's shoulder. Kurt opens his eyes and stares at Tommy in the mirror.

*   *   *

When Tommy wakes up it's dark out and Dan is standing directly outside the open car door by Tommy's feet.

"Hey kid," he says gruffly, his accent somewhere between a Bostonian and an Alabama farmer. "You want somethin' to eat?"

Tommy sits up rubbing his eyes and stretching his back.

"Yeah," he says with a yawn. "Where are we?"

"Arkansas." They had started off in Maryland.

"Cool."

They're parked at a Flying J, one of the many truck stops that line the country's highways. This one looks like they all do, big lit up sign, a huge lot with the capacity to hold three hundred or more trucks. There is a building that features a restaurant, showers, souvenirs and dozens of hardened truckers and travelers who have seen a thousand buildings just like it. But Tommy has never been at a truck stop before. He just looks around in awe.

Dan leads him to a table in the eating section and immediately starts to roll a cigarette from the pouch he has. He does this quickly and with skill, making a perfect cylinder, then licking it sealed and pulling the stray strands of tobacco from one end before sticking it in his mouth and lighting up.

"So, you're going west," he says, letting out a cloud of smoke.

"Yeah, L.A.," Tommy replies, a little more comfortable, but not quite at ease. He takes a cigarette from his pack. It's his last one.

"That's a weird city, you know anyone there?"

"No." They both mull this over for a second, blowing smoke rings. A waitress trots over. She's a nice looking Indian girl, or she usually was. Right now, there's a layer of sweat on her brow and one of her nails is broken.

"Yeah, we'll have two Buds and a chicken dinner, ma'am," Dan tells her. "That ok with you, Tom?" Tommy nods his head to agree. The waitress leaves, still writing in her little pad.

"So how 'bout you?" asks Tommy. "Where are you headin'?"

"Texas. I live there. Got a glass blowing business."

"Sounds good."

"It isn't bad. Keeps the bills paid." The food arrives. The chicken is okay, the beer is better. Tommy practically sucks it down in one gulp. Dan takes a little longer. A bite of chicken then a swig of beer followed by another bite and so on until his plate is clean and his bottle is empty.

5.

As they're leaving the place a long-haired hippie guy with black dreads and leather vest approaches them.

"Hey, you guys spare a little change for gas? Me and my old lady are trying to go east." Dan reaches in his pocket. The hippie takes the bills without even looking at them.

"Every little bit helps, man, thank you my brother." He ambles off to the corner of the building. As they walk away, they can hear him ask the same question and then a muted cuss. Tommy looks back to see a red-faced, balding man walk away angrily. The hippie spreads his arms and says something Tommy can't hear.

"I wish I had more to give that guy," says Dan. "Hell, I've been in that situation more times than I can count."

*   *   *

When they get back to the oversized jeep, Dan throws a bag of weed into Tommy's lap.

"Roll one up, man," he says. Tommy grins despite himself, the bud looks pretty green. He sticks his fingers in to grab a few. Dan starts the car.

"There's a tray on the floor you can roll on and flip down the mirror on the sun shade." Tommy does everything he tells him and pretty soon he's breaking up the buds into the papers he finds in the shade. There's a surprisingly small amount of seeds in the mix. Tommy wonders if the guy is more than just a glass blower. Maybe a drug runner. That would fit the description of anyone dressed the way he was. Almost as though he's reading his thoughts, Dan starts talking.

"Yeah, I always bring a little green with me on these trips, I mean driving forever, no stops. Just gas stations and maybe a little food... you go crazy if you can't relax a little ya'know..."

"You're telling me," says Tommy quickly, piling the marijuana into a paper. It's an incidental comment because Dan just keeps on going anyway.

"When I was coming up from Austin, I actually brought a quarter-pound with me and some bowls I'd blown, sold them to some of my friends and family, y'know. I got enough money to get back out. It only takes a max of two hundred bucks to get cross country, y'know, and only a couple days." He glances over at Tommy. "You finished with that?" he asks. Tommy holds it up. "Right on, spark it up." Tommy does.

"This your first time goin' cross?"

"Yeah," affirms Tommy letting out a pungent cloud of smoke, feelings his muscles relax into a somewhat contented state. "I'm pretty excited."

"Right on, man, I remember when I first hit the road, must have been ten years ago, I was nineteen." Tommy hands over the joint and Dan quickly puts it to his lips.

"You're twenty-nine, man?" Dan takes the joint from his mouth and nods solemnly.

"I know man, I never expected it. Did you know Jim Morrison, Jimmy Hendrix and Janice Joplin all died when they were twenty-seven?" Dan pulls on the cigarette paper again and starts to cough.

"Fuckin' A, everyone knows that." This isn't said offensively, just a fact that Tommy was somehow there to give... wow... this is good pot!

"Yeah, man, and the thing is that at twenty-eight your entire life changes." Dan's voice is muffled by another bout of coughing.

"What?"

"Yeah, man, at twenty-eight everything is turned around. Just ask anyone who's older than twenty-seven." He takes another hit.

"Shit, so they only had to wait another year?" Dan nods in a sagely manner. Tommy wonders if he practices that. Dan hands him the joint and then releases his breath all out in a long line.

"Hell, I never thought I'd be where I am now. When I left, I had nothing and nobody. Just a sleeping bag and somebody stole that from me in the first couple days. Now I got a business, girl-friend, even a dog. She's at home in Texas. She's too old to travel a lot now. She's big, husky and a quarter-wolf. Hell, I think they'd arrest me in Massachusetts for her." It takes Tommy a moment to realize he's talking about his dog and not his girlfriend. The weed is good. Dan seems to be enjoying it.

"That's cool, man," Tommy says, mostly because he can't think of anything else. "That's really cool."

"Fuckin' A, man, fuckin' wicked cool," Dan suddenly grins and hesitantly, Tommy lets his own bust out. It was funny how a good time with a complete stranger in a strange place in the middle of the night can turn out alright. The joint goes back and forth a few times before it gets too small to hold without burning fingers. Dan stubs it out and then puts it in his pocket.

"I mean shit," Dan tells him. "Does happen. Fuckin' can't get a ride. The law got it in for you. Fuckin' courts don't even give you a fair say. Lots of times I can't even get a real meal, just gotta buy Ramen noodles at the Safeway. Hell, I remember one time in Pensacola I was seeing this girl, Brenda, and we were sitting on this beach when this big, beach cop, guy walks up and starts to hassle us, 'cause we got long hair and look dirty and all that…"

Dan tells his story and Tommy listens, but only with half an ear because many times Dan goes into long tangents that have nothing to do with the story. Tommy has a short attention span in any case.

"Anyway, we made bail, but we never went back for the court date, we gave them fake names anyway and plus we knew we wouldn't get a fair shake. Especially seeing as the cop planted the drugs on us in the first place…"

"Another time I remember I was hitchhiking and this guy pulls out this great, fat blunt and we started smoking, but I guess he never thought to tell me they had another couple pounds on the backseat under these blankets. Anyway, when it was my turn to drive some cops pulled us over. Now, I didn't have a license, no registration, so when the cops came to the window I just sort of smiled and tried to talk myself out of it. This was in Kentucky, the summer time and everyone was sweating. Anyway, eventually they asked if they could search the car and I didn't know we had anything substantial, so I said sure. They brought a couple of dogs and everything By this time one of the dudes had told me the score and I was pissed 'cause if I'd known there was that much pot in the car, I would've stashed it when we got pulled over, but no, it was right under the blankets on the backseat..."

"Well, the dogs went in, the dogs came out and they didn't make a sound, now how's that for luck?" Dan looks over to him to see if he's paying attention, the premature wrinkles on his forehead and eyes winking in question. Tommy looks back at him and nods hurriedly like he's only been waiting for Dan to look over.

"Hey, think I can have a cigarette out of your pouch? I'm all out of Marlboros," he asks. In response Dan throws his pouch over onto Tommy's lap.

"Roll another joint while you're at it, we'll wait another hour before smoking it… damn we're making good time. I've never got this far, this fast before." Tommy nods his head obediently and rolls the joint first, then a cigarette. He lights the cigarette, takes a drag and immediately coughs hard.

"Shit," he whispers.

"Yeah, they get some getting used to, but they're the only way to smoke when you're poor."

"It tastes like shit!"

"Well, fuck man, if you don't like it, you don't have to smoke it, but it's the only tobacco in this car." Tommy takes the hint and keeps puffing at the butt. Dan reaches over to turn on the radio and quickly flips through the stations until an Eagles song plays through, then he picks a cigarette off the dashboard that he had rolled earlier. For a long time neither of them say anything. They smoke quietly until the song ends and an annoying car salesman comes over the station.

"Buy now and there will be no interest for the rest of the…" Dan shuts off the radio and shrugs apologetically.

"Sorry, this thing only has a radio, it's annoying as fuck." Tommy agrees with him and asks the first thing that comes to mind.

"So, what kind of music you like?"

"Classic rock mostly, y'know, Doors, Jefferson Airplane, Led Zeppelin, Black Sabbath… You?"

"Grunge, Nirvana mostly. Alice in Chains… I like Neil Young too and some Beatles…"

"Oh yeah, Nirvana. They're not bad. I mean they're not great, but they're better than a lot of the bands in the last decade, y'know."

"Nirvana rocks, man," Tommy tells him.

"Yeah, yeah, I guess they do, fuck load better than all that eighties metal shit, those guys just didn't get it, grunge is a big fuckin' step from that. Gotta wonder how long it'll last though."

They fall silent again while Tommy wonders about that last comment. Dan turns on the radio again and turns it to some modern rock station. Immediately a track from Nevermind comes up.

"There you go kid, a present from me to you." There's a hint of a patronizing tone in his voice, but Tommy ignores it. Nobody is perfect after all. He asks Dan if they can smoke the joint now.

"Hell, it's close enough to an hour, fire it up!" And so, he does.

*   *   *

The girl comes running out onto the dusty Southwestern road. A big blue van bears down on her. Her eyes are fixed on a big blue, red and white beach ball bouncing into the road ahead of her. The shadow's long and dark on the asphalt as the sun's rays flash into the driver's eyes, casting the road into a white blur. When the van hits the little girl's head twists off its axis like a bolt on a screw. Blood coats the road, running towards the sides on the street. The van screeches to a stop with a sickening squish sound that is louder than everything else except for the scream of a young, redheaded mother, running out of the house, wracked with horror and loss. The driver sobs behind the wheel while the radio blares a popular song. There is no one else there and the sky is clear. The sun bears down on the collapsed figures on the road.

*   *   *

By the time Dan and Tommy come onto the scene everything is finished. Someone has presumably called the police.

"Shit, is that a dog" asks Dan with vomit in his throat. Tommy catches a glimpse of a white dress with blue flowers on it.

"No, man, that's a little girl." He whispers.

"Christ," chokes Dan. He slows down and tries to go around.

"Do you think we should pull over?" asks Tommy. Dan gazes at the scene and he looks like he's going to be sick.

"No man, we need to get out of here. There's some things you just shouldn't see." Just then a skinny Mexican boy in all black jumps out of the van and hops over to Dan's window.

"Hey brother," he says and there's no trace of sickness in his voice. "Do you think you can help me out? I was just hitching with this girl. I don't want to get in any trouble and the cops are already on their way." Dan nods weakly. Obviously, he just wants to get out of there. Tommy stares out the window over the boy's head to the mother bawling over the broken girl and at the blonde twenty-something bawling in the van. The sirens are slowly flowing into the scene from far away. Coming closer. By this time a couple of other cars are behind them. Some people pull over to help or just gawk. One guy starts to direct traffic.

"I guess so," says Dan, still shaken. "I'm not going very far, I was going to drop off this kid at the interstate." The boy flashes a smile to Tommy and gets in the back. Tommy keeps staring straightforward as they drive away. His fingers itch, but he can't move them. Somewhere inside is a screaming animal, but all Tommy can do is purse his lips, tongue against the top of his mouth.

PART II

1.

"So, is this stuff good?"

"Oh yeah, shit, man, you can't find anything better than this! Don't worry, man, I wouldn't rip you off!"

Tommy holds the bag under the stupid kid's nose. He's a real custy, about sixteen. Naïve. Obviously has money to spend. Only the rich are so careless about their drug purchases.

The custy has a red, greasy face with freckles and a crew cut. His eyebrows are really dark, like someone filled them in with a black marker and every other second, they crease up as he thinks about the offer. Tommy hates his guts. Very hesitant, the custy hands over a few bills and Tommy drops the bag onto the grass. This is in a small park that is well known for drug distribution. Custies can get anything from a dime bag to a vial of acid here and the dealers range from old hippies to punk kids.

The custies are all alike though. Stupid and nervous. Irritating. What this kid is getting is little more than crushed up aspirin and pot resin. Tommy's calling it opium. Not a bad high if you don't know what you're doing. With any luck, this kid will be back again.

"Cool bro," Tommy slaps the kid's hand and gets up to walk down the street. The kid watches Tommy's back then gets up and walks in the opposite direction. Tommy smiles to himself.

He's been living in the city of L.A. for four months now and he has it all down. Look out for the law. Ask for change and shoplift. Sell real drugs when you got 'em. Sell fake ones when you can get away with it. This time he got away with it, but if he had to, he could handle any disagreement. His appearance is slightly less weighty since he left home. His hair is greasier and tangled. His face is smaller. His eyes are bigger. Bulging out of his sockets. But, despite all this, he is stronger.

He shakes a lot more. That's to be expected. Even though he's been living here, he doesn't really have anywhere to live. He's another of those street kids that survive in every major city and he's proud of that distinction. Recently, he's been thinking of moving on. Maybe go to Mexico or Oregon, but these thoughts are all peripheral because it's really hard to think about anything but the present moment. The day to day. This is especially true when he wakes up under a bridge and immediately has to scrub up some change for breakfast. These days though, that's less and less. Slowly but certainly, he's developing a schedule.

Life's not too bad. He's a good-looking kid. People take pity for his youth and he can make enough money to get food just for asking. His frame and features have matured and when he gets cleaned up he looks just like any college kid in the town but cleaning up is the last thing on his mind today. Right now, he's on his way to Zeke's house to score his own drugs and these ones won't be fake.

What's happened to this child is freedom. Freedom from parents, peers, teachers and priests. He no longer lives by the clock, but by the calendar. He whistles as he walks, just a mile. He has a canteen and he sips it. All the way home, he thinks.

Zeke's house is just a little box in the center of a dozen other little boxes just like it. The ground here is concrete. Desert sand mixes with grains of broken glass and plastic over its surface. The only thing that grows are prickly little desert plants. A few cacti are set up like flower gardens surrounding the houses. The sideboards of this house are painted blue and worn down so the aged wood shows. Around the small lot is a white fence with a broken gate. The lawn is filled with a pink flamingo ornament and little garden gnomes. All in all, it looks like any other house on the block. Just another normal American home.

On closer inspection though, the simple, domestic surroundings are a little more sinister. For one thing, the flamingo has a Mohawk and sunglasses. Half of it is painted black. As for the gnomes, they're lined up on a ledge in front of a concrete wall that has spotted bullet-holes and the ground is covered with broken gnome heads and old shells. All the curtains are closed and the air conditioner emits a steady drone that barely covers the sounds of a Nine Inch Nails album blaring from inside the house.

When Tommy arrives it's about three o'clock. He can tell by the position of the sun, give or take an hour or so. As he opens the gate, a cool, but dry desert breeze picks up and throws dust into his face. He's spitting and shaking his head as he knocks on the door.

The music cut off. A skinny twenty-something with a shaved head and a pale complexion cracks the door. He looks suspiciously at Tommy.

"Hey Mike," Tommy offers this polite greeting with a little wave. Mike stares at him for another minute, then opens the door. Holding his head and a cigarette with one hand, he lets Tommy in.

"Is Zeke here, man?"

Mike nods and just then Zeke walks out of the bedroom. He sits on the one easy chair in the house. The rest of the furniture includes a futon that's done up to look like a couch and a beanbag chair. There's a small TV that Zeke bought from a local fencer, but it's old and isn't used all that much except to watch movies and play video games. The walls of the house are punked out. There's graffiti and drawings all over, most of them are classic like GOD IS GAY and SEX PISTOLS. Interestingly, the floors are almost totally clear of debris, just a very clean gray carpet and one or two of the drawings are pretty good and untouched by any scribbles or rude messages.

Zeke is an older man with spiky, black patches of hair and no cultivated facial hair except for a dark five o'clock shadow that makes him look at once villainous and pathetic. He can't be older than thirty, but he looks like a burnt remnant with more than his share of wrinkles and faded tattoos. Right now, he isn't wearing anything but a pair of leather pants and a studded belt. His chest is sagging, but not quite out of shape. The crooks of his elbows are spotted with needle marks. He's got blue eyes and he grins lop-sidedly. He slaps Tommy on the back as the boy draws near to the chair.

"Hey mate," he says, an English accent still discernible after years in this country, "Whadaya need? Coke?"

"Uh, actually I was hopin' I could buy some dope off you," Tommy says suddenly a little nervous. He wasn't a stranger to hard drugs, but this was his first foray into the world of heroin. He promised himself he wouldn't develop a habit and he'd successfully kept cocaine a party drug.

So, there was that…

Maybe he is cutting it close, maybe it's too much of a risk, but he isn't going to deny himself the experience. The thing is, living on the streets without seeing the sad wrecks of heroin junkies every day is like living with eyes closed, but on the other hand, not one of them could deny the incredible high. A little change of pace, thinks a nervous Tommy. It's obvious that Zeke is surprised by the request, but he recovers quickly and slaps Tommy on the back again.

"Hey man, no problem, guess we can't call you Tommy Cocaine anymore, aye? This is for yourself, right? You need a place to shoot up?"

"Uh, yeah."

"Well, make yourself at home, I'll mix up the shot and I'll tell you what," he smiles. "First one's on the house." Zeke pulls Tommy into the kitchen and sits him at the table, then goes into the bathroom to get things ready all the while whistling some tune and babbling encouragements, most of which are unintelligible.

"Zeke sure loves turning people onto dope," Mike observes grimly. Tommy smiles in a fit of nervousness. Something about

Mike always bothers Tommy. He just seems so numb. From another world. There was this way that he stares. His eyes are so dark and his pupils are almost always pinned and they just stand there motionless, focused on nothing but the face in front of them. The way he stares… it's like he can kill a man without feeling even one pang of guilt. It isn't that he is scary-looking, or tough, or was even prone to violence, but he scares Tommy. There is just the sense that he isn't all there and what is isn't entirely human. Tommy searches his mind for something to say to break that stare.

Zeke pops out of the bathroom holding a syringe and grinning ear to ear.

"Let's have it on, aye?"

2.

A lone. The feeling that overcomes all other senses lasts only a moment before a silent rush fills his brain. Coming up from what seemed a great depth, he thinks he can see a face. It's slowly making its way upward to him. Becoming more distinct. Soft features of cheeks and chin come along with a cool, piercing look of openness. Almost blue eyes that seem to strike faster than anything that Tommy has felt before as he moves upward. Away.

"Just so," says a voice that Tommy has learned to be Kurt's. "Just like a moon flake off some star." The voice trails off as if singing and Tommy moves. He moves upward and with might. It's a long time before he opens his eyes,

"Good then?"

Zeke hovers above him in a halo of sunshine. Tommy can't tell where the light's coming from. The room hadn't been bright when he fell into… well, whatever. Tommy decides that heroin isn't as much as he'd hoped.

Suddenly he feels his insides rumble and Tommy jumps up. Zeke watches him run to the bathroom.

Pain. Searing, beautiful pain. Like a lightning bolt of sensation of fear, suspicion, greed and lust all rolled up into one. He pukes his guts up into the toilet.

He doesn't die of embarrassment.

Tommy wipes the vomit from his face and tries to run the sink to wash his face and hands. Things seem so surreal, all of a sudden. Like the day had been made again and again and again and he is watching it all.

Creation, destruction, creation, destruction. The world spins and orbits and crashes like dying waves on a coast a long way from here.

Tommy sits back into a chair in the living room with the comforting thought that Hampton Beach would be opening up soon under its cool, cloudy spring day.

Zeke says something.

"So, you wanna 'nother load there, pal?" he asks quizzically. Tommy shakes his head. He can't seem to talk, his mind's all dried up and the rest of him wasn't listening anyway.

"How do you do it?" Tommy asks, finally. The words coming out of his mouth in slow motion. "It's… it's incredible."

"Don't know," Zeke replies. "Somehow the stuff just stays in me." He slaps his leather covered thighs.

"You can hang out for a couple of hours before Sisi gets home," he says. "But then I gotta kinda kick you out. Sisi doesn't like a lot of visitors."

Tommy nods and slowly turns into the plush armchair. "I won't be a bother," he says, "Just wake me up when it's time to go."

He falls back, eyes open wide watching Zeke walk into the kitchen and then somehow appear on the wall dancing slowly like a gigantic kind of bird. On the television, a group of men talk around a campfire and a sound of music spears its way into his waiting mind.

That was all.

*   *   *

When Tommy comes back to himself he is on a beach. The sun has set below the waves and the sand is getting cool to the touch. Several yards away on his right is a campfire sputtering up red flames and embers. A few figures stand around it holding beer and cigarettes. Tommy pulls his jacket out of his pack and buries himself inside of it as the water soaks the heat from the land. It had been so amazing. Like life itself sucking away from him, but Tommy wants it again. He examines this desire as he pats out a cigarette out of his pack of Marlboros.

Again and again. He thinks to himself like some kind of caged rodent, trying to figure out how to get another piece of cheese. The path to the beach had been strange. Starting from the doorstep of Zeke's house, over the highway, to the bus stop and then suddenly on the bus with all its strange sounds and the differences of the rocky, sandy landscape outside…

"Ahh," a voice sounded. Tommy looks up to see Arab standing behind him. "He wakes, he sees," says Arab. Tommy sighs and takes a drag off his smoke.

Arab is a large, black man of Jamaican origin. Or so he says. What Arab says vaguely makes sense to Tommy. That's how all things seem with Arab. Just enough to be believable. Nothing of substance to latch onto and create a living, breathing story. Perhaps it was his way of being mysterious. Keeping secrets.

"Ah, he comes to life again," Arab intones.

"Hey 'Rab," says Tommy.

Arab was the first person Tommy met in L.A. It had been when he was waiting for his traveling companion who was in one of the many shops lining Santa Monica.

"Ah," Arab had said. "Another little bird bearing tidings from? The East, the west? No." He smiled. "To the west there is only waves and beyond that a little land. This bird must've come from…" He stopped suddenly without hesitating as though his words made as much sense as they needed to. And they did. Arab thought Tommy was from Seattle.

Just then Tommy's copilot, Joe, walked out.

"C'mon," said Joe, looking rather pissed off. "We're done here." Tommy picked up the backpack they'd bought in Texas and strolled behind Joe. Arab had stood through it all, eyes closed and arms held horizontal in front of him.

Now Arab stands much the same way, but Tommy isn't feeling it. He mutters something almost complementary then rises up.

"Ahh," says Arab. "Is the little bird heading south for winter? For summer?"

Nothing Arab says put Tommy at ease. There's a tension inside him like his organs were leaking their way out of his skin. Nothing that couldn't be cured with beer, thinks Tommy and he pushes himself away. Arab doesn't say a word.

The fire is surrounded by about ten people. Mostly white with a few black people and one Hawaiian as far as Tommy can

see. They have a cooler full of beer. Tommy instinctively walks
towards it. It's probably the most rude thing someone can do, but
what can anyone expect? He's on drugs.

"Hey man," says one white boy with a flat nose and a polo
shirt on. "What's up?"

Tommy doesn't really know how to respond. The back of his
teeth itch.

"Hey," he says and then sort of looks down. "You guys looked
like you were having fun so I thought…"

He trails off, but as he looks up he sees the boy is smiling.
Tommy grumbles for a moment, suddenly ashamed of his torn
jeans and stained white T-shirt.

"That's cool, dude," says the boy. "More the merrier," he reaches into the cooler and pulls out a Budweiser. "Help yourself," he
explains. Tommy looks up, grateful for the company.

"I'm Tommy," he says and then opens the can. "I'm… I'm not
really from around here…"

"That's cool, Tommy. Where you from? Do you go to school
around here?"

"No," Tommy shakes his head. "I'm from Boston." He takes
a swig of the beer he's holding. It really did feel good, like he was
stepping into the real world from a horrid dream. "I just sort of,
y'know, came out to see L.A…."

"Awesome man," says the boy. "I'm Ben. It's a pleasure to meet
you. We got plenty of sorts here." He looks around and bends
down slightly to say something in a whisper. "It's the fire that
brings them out."

As it turns out, three of the guys, all college students, had come out to the beach with a cooler. Some more of their friends showed up and then a few beachcombers had arrived once the fire was crackling. Tommy had been the last of them. He takes a seat by the fire and feels truly warm for the first time in months. The figure beside him turns.

"So how 'bout that music, huh?" she says in a friendly tone. "How 'bout that Nirvana?"

"It's good," Tommy says with a half-smile. "They're in a bit of trouble right now."

"Oh right, I know," says the girl who isn't bad looking at all and probably attends a college somewhere in the area. But she is older, probably around 20. Tommy hates to talk to older people. He can get along fine with guys, but he still feels tongue tied while talking to women. They just seem so much wiser and on top of things. Tommy can't even really conceive what he is doing such a long way from home.

The night progresses and the guys go out for another cooler. Apparently, they are all in their last year.

"Y'know, I can't even figure out what's real anymore," says the girl, whose name he learned was Stephanie. She huddles in a sweatshirt around the coals of the fire. "Do you know what I mean?"

"Of course," says Tommy. This encounter is going well and Tommy dreams of a shower and a laundry machine. Fairly soon, they are kissing. Stephanie leads Tommy to her car.

"I haven't done this before," she says. "Have you?"

"No," says Tommy, a little drunk and there was still the heroin to consider.

"I don't want you to think I'm like this all the time," she tells him and it was exactly what Tommy was thinking. This was his first time in L.A. This western experience, he thinks. He'd been in a bunch of hotel rooms, most of them bought by Joe, but, generally speaking, he hadn't been approached in quite this way. The closest was bringing a girl over to a small motel to take a shower and sleep off the streets, but there was nothing physical…

"Y'know, but I don't know when I'll see you again…"

"It's alright, I'll sleep on the couch," says Tommy.

"No, no, no, my roommate would freak out. You'll have to sleep with me…" Tommy shrugs then lowers his head to her lips.

"But nothing, ok," she tells him after she kisses him again. "I'm not that kind of girl."

For all apparent purposes, she is that kind of girl, but Tommy keeps his mouth shut, until he opens it up to her tongue.

"I know," he says, afterwards.

They arrive at her apartment, a tan building with her's on the second floor. Stephanie points to a door.

"That's my roommate. Try to be quiet."

Pretty soon they are making out next to her bed.

"Do you have a condom?" she asks. Tommy pulls one out of his wallet. "No, no. Those aren't any good… here use these." She opens up a drawer and hands him two.

"I think we'll need more, but oh, let's go." The two of them undress each other and Tommy thinks of the bathroom as she heaves and moans underneath him.

"This is the best," she whispers. Tommy wonders if it'd be rude to shower after it was over. Just the booze and the heroin talking again.

3.

The next day Tommy awakes to Stephanie dressing. He lies in bed, watching her pull on jeans and brush her hair.

"I've got to get going," she says. "I don't mean to turn you out..."

"It's alright," says Tommy.

"Here, this is my number and address, you call it any time and we..." She looks up lecherously all of a sudden with some kind of glint in her eyes..

"...we can have some more fun."

She hugs him in the living room, then they kiss in the doorway as she locks the door. "Don't be a stranger," she says and then she's gone. Tommy waits a moment, then follows her from the hallway of the apartment building into the outdoors. He sees her car turn the corner leaving the parking lot.

Great.

Now the only question is: where the hell is he? And how the hell does he get out of here?

*   *   *

It hadn't always been that way. After Dan dropped them off, east past up bumfuck, Tommy and his new companion had immediately started walking until they reached an onramp. Tommy looked around cautiously then his new "friend" put his pack down. Tommy still only possessed the shirt on his back.

"So," said the kid.

"My name's Tommy," Tommy said, extending a hand.

"Joe," said the boy. "It's a pleasure, I'm sure."

"That whole wreck?"

"All behind me, I swear. Don't even think about it."

"That girl…"

"All behind me, I swear."

"I think she died, I can't…" Tommy suddenly had his face in his hands. "I can't…"

"Look!" the boy grabbed Tommy's palms. "It's gone. It happened and it's over. We gotta stay cool and figure this out!"

"I can't! That girl! It's too much, I'm just…" Just then a police siren blared behind them. "Oh shit, shit, shit…"

"Hello boys," said the officer, getting out of his squad car. "What're we up to today?"

"Um," said Tommy.

"Just traveling, sir," said Joe. The cop came closer.

"Anything dangerous in that bag?" he asked, very politely.

Tommy looked at Joe and tightened his lips to keep from screaming. Joe kind of smiled as he shook his head. "Nothing at all, sir," he said.

"Nothing? No bullets, guns, grenades?"

"I wouldn't know anything about those, sir."

"Well, it can't hurt to be careful," the cop stopped short to look towards the sun. "Where are you headed?"

"L.A., sir."

"Well, I can give you a ride to our local truck stop, but I'll have to search you. No knives, points, sharps in your pockets?"

"No, sir."

"Well, it can't hurt to be sure."

The cop gestured to the car and Joe lurched over to it and spread his arms over the top.

"Nothing wrong, sir," he said evenly. The cop worked his way around Joe's limbs. After a moment, he was done. He turned to Tommy.

"Your turn, son."

Tommy felt like screaming. The whole world was coming apart along the seams of his face. He blinked once. Soon tears were going to start rolling down from his eyes. The cop, silent, performed a very professional search.

"Put the bag into the trunk, son," said the cop to Joe when it was over. "Sorry, state laws."

Joe looked into the very large trunk as if he wondered if he'd fit into it as well. Then he walked back to the front of the car.

Before very long the trio were on the highway. Tommy wondered what interstate they were on and where that put them on the map. Joe sat solemnly in his seat. Just stared forward. Occasionally, he scratched his nose.

"You boys be careful now," said the policeman as he let them out. The truck stop looked the same as any other. Tommy glanced at the front of the cop's car. It said Texas.

The police drove away and Joe picked up his bag then,

without a word, walked to the restaurant next to the big wheel-ers. Tommy followed. They walked inside. Joe moved towards a booth in the interior, looking around and smiling while Tommy followed feeling cold and miserable. The trip wasn't going as planned.

They found a booth. A green, plush one with a tear in the center bottom. Nobody else had taken it till Tommy and Joe sauntered in. They sat down. For a few minutes neither said any-thing, just sort of looked at each other without being able to see. Finally, a waitress arrived.

"Coffee?" she asked. Both nodded. She placed menus before each of them and walked back behind the counter. Presumably to get the coffee. Joe spoke first.

"So…" he said. Tommy stared down at his menu.

"Where are you going?" he finished.

"L.A.," mumbled Tommy.

"Great, that's where I'm headed. I just drove from Miami…"

"That girl…"

"My ex-girlfriend, just helpin' me out."

"No, I mean…"

"That's over." Tommy looked up to find Joe staring him di-rectly in the eye. Tommy couldn't handle the gaze so he looked at the menu again.

"Right," he mumbled.

"I guess you want to know what I'm doing."

Tommy shrugged, but Joe continued without noticing.

"I'm in the runner business."

Tommy shrugged again. Nothing Joe said could surprise him and he wasn't really listening.

"That van," he leaned in close. "Was full of weed."

Tommy looked up again. A rising feeling of hatred started to glow in his eyes and it traveled straight from his backbone to his brain.

"Really?" he said finally.

"Yup. Here in my pack," Joe explained. "Is about ten kilos of cocaine."

Tommy took all this in and looked around to see if anyone was listening. He wanted to knock the tanned face of Joe right off, but it wasn't the time.

"Um," he said.

"So, you can see the kind of fix I'm in."

Tommy nodded.

"Listen, I don't want to hassle you. I'm twenty years old and I can tell when I'm not welcome, but you're in a bit of trouble yourself. You think every cop you'll bump into will be Mr. Jolly like that last freak? I'm tellin' you, it's statistically impossible. This is your first time out, isn't it? I can tell. You still have baby fat. So, like me or not, you're stuck with me and that's fine. I'll bring you to L.A. I'll get you sorted out."

Tommy didn't want to describe himself as "not-liking" Joe. He loathed Joe. He transcended hatred into a pile of cold rage that beat in time with his heart.

"So, yeah," he said, not really meaning anything. Moments passed. Tommy looked up just as the waitress placed a cup of coffee in front of him. He tried to smile. The kid had just walked away, he was thinking, just walked away without looking sick at all, this motherfucker, this piece of shit...

"A plate of large fries," said Joe.

"That it?" asked the waitress.

"Yeah," said Joe.

"Alrighty then, that'll be just a minute," she walked off again holding the pot of coffee. Joe turned his attention back to Tommy. After a moment, Tommy spoke.

"Alright," he said, "You're right, what do we do now?"

"Well, now we eat," said Joe. "Then later on I'll try to get us a straight ride to the city." He looked pointedly at Tommy then sipped his black coffee. "Do you understand?"

Tommy nodded, his hatred easing out of him. Above all Tommy considered himself a pragmatist. What Joe said made sense. What the hell did Tommy know about traveling? And Texas held a sort of dread that diverted all his instincts that stood against Joe's offer. There were stories and then there were stories. We're stuck, he thought.

Part of him knew that this was a bad idea. The cops would probably be looking for Joe in connection with the crash. What if they found him? With all the drugs he claimed to have on him? What would they say Tommy was? An innocent bystander? An accomplice?

Tommy knew all this, but it only propelled him forward. What he wanted was to simply get out of there and never come back. Quickly, if that was at all possible. What he didn't want was to be lynched by a mob of Yankee hating rednecks. The part of him that knew this was a bad idea screamed out that this sick bastard only exasperated that situation, but Tommy flatly ignored his own mind.

Instead he played a fast rhythm on his thighs.

"Don't worry," said Joe. "I'll get you sorted out."

4.

Back to now, Tommy manages to find a bus stop by the collegiate apartment complex and wonders where that half Mexican look-alike is. He needs to head back to Santa Monica Pier to meet him. A slow, disconcerting feeling of sickness still remains in his gut, but he ignores it. That'd been a wild night and he didn't care to replay it again. Except the parts with Stephanie. That had been fun. And maybe the parts with the needle and the dope, he admits to himself.

The bus trip is uneventful. Just one transfer needed. That surprises Tommy and he briefly wonders how many boys had found their way into Stephanie's apartment. He thinks of this idly, picking the piece of paper out of his pocket and wondering.

He'll call her tonight, he decides. That'd be acceptable. Maybe they could meet and do the whole thing over again. Maybe this time he could shower. He feels a brief pang in his stomach.

Through the months that Tommy had stayed in L.A. he had managed to pull his anger and hatred of Joe into a small ball that he held casually in his chest. It'd be good to break ties with Joe, but for now Joe was all he had. He'd been the one to find that slightly drunk truck driver in the parking lot. He'd been the one to show him Sunset Boulevard and the Santa Monica strip. He'd shown him how to deal drugs on the street, in an alley, behind a club. The list went on and on. He'd been the one to introduce him to Zeke. After that he'd stayed like he was watching over his own flesh and blood or something.

It couldn't be more absurd, Tommy thinks. The kid is over Tommy's age, but he's shorter, slighter and looks like Tommy's kid brother. Tommy wonders how he got this way. Whether he'd always been this way, but Joe was secretive about his past. It was "all behind him." Tommy couldn't understand that. Sometimes, in the middle of the night, he'd still wake up thrashing, haunted by the memory of soft blue eyes and bloodstained blonde hair.

The plan was to meet at the tall end of the pier and see an already high Zeke, fishing off the end. Not exactly an original idea, but it still beat constantly traveling out to Zeke's house which, as Zeke said, was not a visitor friendly area.

Tommy doesn't understand why Zeke doesn't just cut his hair, clean up his house and suit Joe and him with some nice clothes so they could actually enter the clubs they prowled around at night. It'd be easier and more profitable, but as Zeke put it, he's just holding onto their drugs for which he'd paid a small fortune for and now was doling them out for pennies and quarters as a living.

Zeke had a lot of ideas and dealings, but this one was even a little over the top for Tommy's tastes. Still, each night they'd pay up, spending the majority that was made off the "loan" Zeke had made them in the first place. The initial amount was used to pay off Joe's creditors. So, it must make sense somehow.

The day is beautiful, still a bit cold. It's about seven in the morning. The sun would soon warm up the entire area, but

Tommy took out the jacket from the pack Joe had gotten him. At night, before he's ready to sleep, he'd place the whole sack next to a dumpster and then pick it up later on his nightly scavenger hunt for a place to stay. During the day, he kept it on. It was always good to use it as a prop when he asked the kind people of L.A. for some change to help him out.

Being on the street was like being an actor and Tommy had met several such aspiring young stars doing the same thing as him. They had better haircuts though. And dreams. Tommy listened to them for as long as they cared to talk when they weren't rushing around looking for jobs. He wonders if he should do the same. But he had his business.

Now, though, he just wants to get out of the city. Fuck it all. Maybe head south. Or north. He thinks about home a lot, too, of how much he must have hurt his parents. He misses his sister, the little scamp. The entire essence of the trip had become twisted and distorted. Mostly his misses Gina.

New things are always coming up though, he thinks. As much as he misses Gina and his old life, the new one was insurmountably more interesting.

He'd seen a magician practicing with knives. A big, bulging entertainer with a beard and top hat. Next to him was a young boy, presumably an apprentice, who held the knives and swords for the magician to peruse over as he deliberately pauses before each flourish. Tommy wonders how someone could get into that gig, and remembers having given them a dollar. Tommy considers them to be his kindred, just living in the center of the entire world and making it like it was a child's game.

However, on other days, Tommy sits on the patio of cafés and drinks coffee, watching all the people come and go feeling the sting of jealousy. He'd like to be one of them, someday. Rich and happy. For him, their presence proved there's more to life than rock bottom, more than the street existence he's found himself in.

Yeah. Sure.

Tommy's excited about where life could take him, but he's also scared stiff of what the future might bring. There seems to be a lot of obstacles to really making it in this town. He just has to change what he's been doing, he thinks.

As he rides the bus, he puts on like he likes his life and he wouldn't trade it for anything. The only thing makes him alive is this, he thinks. The only thing that can stop him, is himself and the only thing that really bugs him is his dreams.

Since that day in Texas, the dreams had become more and more vivid. Dark alleys and subway stops. Walking along the highway. In these slumbers it is Kurt Cobain, always Kurt, never the rest of the band or some other rock star who became his constant friend.

He wakes up confused. Maybe Kurt had been explaining the medicinal value of Valium or they'd both been backstage listening to the arguments of the promoter and the manager. Sometimes the two of them would stand for photos, or pull down a fire escape, or sail on a yacht or any number of things. Always ridiculous, but somehow real. Too real. It was beginning to sketch Tommy out.

When Tommy finally makes it to the pier, he's shivering. It's nice out. The air is warm. The sun is shining, but Tommy is dope sick, he thinks. He feels like he's crawling out of his skin. He hopes that seeing Zeke wouldn't trigger another use. Maybe neither of them would say anything and he could continue in his joyful life without becoming a full- blown junkie. It's not worth it, he thinks, but his guts don't want to agree with his head.

Tommy just keeps putting one foot in front of another in the sunny L.A. weather, sidling past tourists taking pictures. There's no way out of this sickness. He just has to deal with it somehow. He doesn't know what he'd been thinking.

As he moves through the human obstacle course, Tommy imagines his heroin addiction to be a lot like a suit of cloth that he can finally fit into. Those rich tourists would have an honest reason to help him out, he thinks, but then recoils in horror at the thought.

Pathetic. That's what he'd be to them, and he'd deserve it.

Tommy imagines the scenario. All day sitting comatose on the sidewalk, drool dripping down his chin. For his nights, he'd sell and use drugs in a frenzy and at the end of the night he'd have absolutely nothing. That is, if he wasn't arrested.

That'd be his life.

He wishes that he had a place to sit and just relax forever and ever, but he squashes that thought, too. Remain busy, that's the ticket. He'd heard a lot over the months from dope-fiends as to how good heroin was and now that he's had a taste, he wants more. Just like all of them. But, he'd been lucky that some of these poor addicts had passed on good intel on what works and what doesn't to kicking the habit entirely. Not that those ever work forever.

Maybe it's just everything he's heard that's making him sick, he thinks, but even imagined pain is still pain. These are baby dope withdrawals, he says to himself. Nothing like the real thing.

He'll just have to handle it, he finally resolves. He understands another shot will send him over the edge. Just like these dreams, the sickness would just have to be dealt with.

5.

Zeke isn't even there when he gets to the end of pier, but Joe is. He gives Tommy a little wave as the tall, skinny, long haired youth makes his way towards him.

"How goes it?" Joe asks when Tommy relaxes against the rail. Tommy just nods and puts his chin on his forearms. He stares out into the ocean. Joe looks at him a little queerly then looks out into the endless horizon with him. For a few minutes neither of the pair speaks. It can't last forever though. Tommy felt his knees shivering while Joe looks idly on.

"So, you tried it?" Joe asks quietly.

"Yeah," says Tommy.

"And?"

"Incredible."

"Yeah, my ex was into that shit. She rode off with some supplier years ago. For all I know, she's turning the same tricks somewhere far off. Believe me, it's not worth it."

Tommy feels his heart beating a thousand miles a second. He opens his lips, but no sound comes out of them. He feels like he is the damned come back to life. It would not surprise him if Joe offered him a jugular vein to quench his intolerable thirst for life, energy, heroin.

"Yeah," he says softly.

"Well, that's it, you haven't been on it long, have you? Zeke stopped by about twenty ago, I got the stuff. We're good to go for the night."

"Yeah." Again, very softly.

"You want some breakfast?" Tommy shakes his head. He didn't feel like he could stomach it. All he wants is more heroin. He suddenly realizes this is what it's like to be a homeless junkie. It's cruel, cold and more like life than he'd ever given it credit for.

"Yeah," he says for a third time, then falls from the railing onto the pier. "I can't do this today, I don't think…"

"You'll be fine. Wanna go downtown?"

"I guess."

"You'll be fine," Joe says again. "In fact, you might make more. If you don't mind, I'll be getting the stuff from now on. I don't think you can handle Zeke."

"I'll be fine," Tommy says with a little bit of vomit in his throat. "I'm not some junkie."

"Hey, it's up to you. I'm just trying to look out for you."

"It's ok. I just had to learn this… for myself."

"I guess, so. Be careful though… I'm just worried."

Tommy thinks about how many times he's felt like belting Joe in the face, but for some reason the rage isn't in him now. He isn't sure if it's the drugs or whether he'd genuinely started to like Joe. He is, after all, the only friend in this strange place he'd come into. However, he is also being an annoying nag.

"Don't worry," Tommy says.

If the beach on Santa Monica can be called crowded, at least it was consistent. The downtown was either a ghostly village, or a seething metropolis of self-endowed super men and women depending when you got there. Joe and Tommy get there on a busy beat and immediately sit next to a building. They look dirty, Tommy especially and they put their packs down as seats.

"Spare some change, sir," asks Joe, saying it again and again as the people passing toss nickels and quarters and sometimes dollars into the hat that lay at their feet. In front of the hat there is a small sign that reads "HELP THE HOMELESS" on it. There isn't a lot of irony in this day's event. They had no money and the strangers who saw them did.

Gradually, the laws of equilibrium had to shift. So, after a half hour passes they count their earnings and find that they've accumulated about twenty dollars. It isn't a lot of money compared to what could be made at the park, but Joe has some rules about schedule and predictability of movement. He gets up and stretches.

Tommy had all this time been bent over his knees alternatively staring out at the ground or closing his eyes. He really feels miserable and, for the first time, he has a genuine feeling of gratitude to his 'patrons.'

"This fucking blows!" Joe says suddenly and picks up his pack. "Let's find somewhere else, I think the cops got a bead on us and besides we can get something to eat and take a shower at the truck stop."

Tommy's perpetually gloomy face begins to brighten up the tiniest amount. "Actually," he says with a kind of smirk. "I'm all set on that."

"What, so you wanna go somewhere else?"

"No, no, let's just get something to eat around here, maybe head to beach, sunbathe…" Tommy had always felt he should enjoy L.A. like a tourist on his first trip. Joe hates him for it. There's something about a code or at least some guidelines that he felt they should model their life after. People want to see rich, successful alcoholics on vacation, not dirty scumbags, he's said. Tommy figures Joe'd been in the drug business for too long. He's beginning to take on the custies' stupid morals.

"I know a place we could hang out for awhile," Joe says.

"Good enough for you, I want to soak in the sun." Tommy doesn't even know where these words are coming from. They were like some kind of deep embedded command inside him somewhere. He thinks, maybe it was just because he got laid the night before. He feels manly and continues to feel that way until he stands up and then feels like he's going to pass out.

"Well, I'll meet you in Hollywood," says Joe gruffly. It was strange how Joe lived. Tommy believes he is looking for another big break like the one he had. But he's stubborn, that was for sure. Guess that's where Tommy's attitude came from too.

"Right," Tommy says weakly. "Just don't be late."

"Same to you."

The first step is getting something to eat. Tommy doesn't want much, just a piece of coffee cake, or whatever it is they're selling in these corner convenient/coffee shop places that seem to be wherever rich business men and women congregate. He gets the pack on his back and walks about three blocks away. He comes into the shop and picks up a piece of bread from the counter, orders a coffee and upon receiving it, sits down at a table opposite of a fan in the corner and tries to ignore the world as he chews.

"This is fuckin' bullshit!" he hears a voice in back of him. "I know when I'm being manipulated and this is fuckin' it!" Tommy turns to see two men in suits sitting opposite each other, half watching the television on the wall and the other half talking. It was some kind of entertainment show. Nothing special. Just glossy and quick like everything in this town.

"All this bullshit over a rock star, like I'm supposed to feel sorry for his rich ass," the man pauses to take a sip of his coffee. Tommy does the same, eavesdropping.

"What's in my head is my personal property," the man continues. "I don't need to be cow-poked into line with all these other punk idiots who act like they're on the edge of the rapture or something."

His friend just sips his coffee and eyes the television as the man let out a few more sentences about mind control and corporate manipulation.

"If I had the power I'd give all sorts of money and women and drugs and whatever he wants," the man says. "But I don't and I'll buy the records I like, thank you very much."

Tommy continues his breakfast, then picks his pack up from the bench he's seated at, wipes his mouth, suppresses the vomit attempting to get up his throat and walks out. Stupid yuppies, he thinks. Why get bent out of shape where twenty dollars was going to go to?

The fact remains that the lead singer of Nirvana and his wife are in the center of a media frenzy because everyone wants to know what the state of their baby is. Tommy doesn't see much in it. It wasn't as though he didn't care, but this constant surveillance is just insane. People got together and made choices and accepted them, learned from them and moved on. There wasn't any need to put it on page one.

Maybe the guy is right and the whole scandal is aimed at giving Nirvana another number one album, he thinks, but it's just people talking. There isn't some kind of corporate agenda that's trying to beat down his mental defenses. It's just the world.

Tommy feels good to know he could at least think along these lines. He'd met a lot of people like that man back there who couldn't discern reality from fantasy. The thing about L.A. is that it attracts a lot of mindsets and that meant coming in contact with some strong opinions. At least this guy didn't think that the President was a servant of Satan.

6.

The beach off the boardwalk is basically deserted when he gets there. A few tourists mill around before getting back to the excitement of stores and entertainment. Tommy squeezes right through the middle of it, takes a towel out of his bag and lies down. This is supposed to make him happy. It doesn't. Somehow though, maybe from the sun, maybe his own inner demons taking hold, he falls asleep.

Inside his head he sees the high ceilings. He's in a warehouse, a large structure. The floor is filled with people. They're dancing.

Tommy walks through them to the stage where three figures are ripping records out of their sleeves. Smiling. Talking to each other. Comparing albums. They are the three members of Nirvana, ripping up the night with their own style of hip hop and R & B.

Tommy can't quite make out their faces, but they're smiling. A girl brushes up beside him and he looks over to see a Hispanic face smiling over at him. He wonders whether he should get out of the way, but before he can move, she reaches out and takes his hands. Then he wakes up.

Tommy knows the girl from the dream. Her name is Sisi and she's basically Zeke's wife. Live in girlfriend might be the better term. She works at a local grocery store near their house and is generally a good person. Tommy doesn't know much about her, except what Zeke had told him. She seems nice.

Suddenly his stomach muscles all cramp at the same time and he's rocking back and forth on the beach. Fuck it, he thinks and drags himself up. He's going to Zeke's house.

The way down to the house is fraught with twists and turns and that's just Tommy's bowels. He leaves the bus in a somewhat uncivil manner as he lurches from it like a drunk cowboy from a wild bronco. Things couldn't get much better.

When he got to the door, Zeke is smiling as Tommy almost tumbles into the house.

"Honey," he yells. "We need a lemonade here!"

Pretty soon he is in the chair looking blindly outward. Zeke is at his side pulling his arm out.

"Ooh, these veins are crying out!"

"I just," Tommy starts. "Want a line. Just something to straighten out…"

"Oh, we'll get you sorted out."

"Just a blow, man," Tommy says weakly. Zeke stops patting his forearm.

"We don't call it a blow," he mumbles. "But if that's what you want…"

"Yeah, it is." Tommy sits up a bit. He wasn't going to turn into a junkie. His eyes burn, his body aches. But he wasn't going to become a junkie. Zeke shrugs. He walks away into his bedroom then comes out with a mirror and a vial.

"This'll sort you out," he mumbles. A crash comes from the

kitchen and Tommy instinctively raises his head towards the doorway.

"Just a minute," Zeke says. Tommy throws his head down, clouding his vision with hair, but it's the pain that mostly blurs it. Why, he thinks, but then another chasm opens beneath him and he feels himself vomiting onto the floor. A muffled curse comes from above.

"Right," Zeke says. He sets the mirror on the table and walks away. Tommy's eyes roll back into his head. He feels Zeke beside him again.

"Sorry, man, but it's for the best. We'll make a comedown plan right after this, I swear."

Tommy tries to shake him off, but he can't move a muscle. The world has burst. Slowly, Tommy feels his vision tunnel, then widen. His muscles relax, his stomach stops hurting. It was instantaneous.

"Thanks," he says, then he falls asleep.

*   *   *

He's back in the warehouse, the lights are flooding hypnotically with the beat of the music. Tommy finds himself dancing. He's waving his hands in the air and laughing insanely. Things are going to get better, in fact, things are going great.

*   *   *

When he wakes up, the first thing he sees is Zeke passed out on the couch. It's getting dark outside so he picks his pack off the floor. He feels alright, nothing special, but he feels ok. The house lights are off, but there's some movement in the kitchen. As he walks to the bathroom a head pops out.

"Oh hey," she says.

"Hey," says Tommy, not knowing what to say.

"You..."

"I'm ok," Tommy runs a hand through his hair. "Really."

"Not surprised, Zeke should be a nurse."

"Yeah, um, I guess."

"Just don't puke next time."

"I'll try not to."

"Great," she smiles suddenly. "Well, bye."

"Bye."

*   *   *

Tommy always thought the streets of Hollywood would be lit up to their brightest, but on a Wednesday night there is barely anything going on, just a few clubs open on the Strip. After getting out of the subway he pulls a cigarette out of his pocket and lights up. He hasn't smoked for about two days and he still has some Marlboros. His lifestyle affords him that.

He doesn't see Joe around anywhere, but that was alright, they rarely met up before the first sale. Quietly Tommy pushes his pack under the dumpster of one of the clubs, then stands up and tries to appear normal. It doesn't take very long before Joe shows up.

"Shit man," he says. "You look terrible."

It's true, there are puke stains on his jeans, his eyes are pinned, his entire body screams out for examination. He isn't what exactly incognito.

"You're alright," Joe says. "Here's the money from the first sale and some change… fuck it, just give them each a teenth. I'll be around." The money and drugs exchange hands and Joe makes his farewell. Tommy slumps next to the wall as Joe goes out of sight. This was how things went. Joe found the customers, sent them back to the alley after some money passed hands and Tommy sold the drugs in the alley. It was strange because the club goers had to pay twice just to get their fix often enough, but they really didn't seem to care. It was all part of security.

If it was a big dude, Joe would escort them to the alley, but mostly it was young, nicely dressed middleweights that came down the alley and Tommy was more than glad to give them what they needed. For a price.

So, a few custies come and go. Tommy is actually feeling pretty good. The desert air is doing wonders, he thinks, momentarily forgetting the load of chemicals in his veins. He is just thinking of turning it in when Joe suddenly appears at the end of the alley. With him is a large heavily tattooed man.

"This is great," he says. "You guys got a great organization. I like that, you should be working for me and my boys."

"We'd appreciate anything at all," Joe says, flashing a smile mostly for Tommy's benefit, "We sure would."

"Great, then I'll take whatever you have. I'll see you tomorrow."

"Sure thing."

Tommy digs the rest of the drugs out of his pockets and the big man grins. Joe grins a lot too, but he is always smiling during a deal. Nothing excites Joe more than moving upward on the drug ladder. Most of the time he'd hit a dead end, just a rich user who liked to hang out, but apparently sometimes it worked out. Zeke, for instance.

Tommy doesn't know what Joe's supplier had thought of the botched road trip, but Joe never mentioned it and it seems to have blown over. For all intents and purposes, Tommy would rather just stay low. Nobody messes with him, not even the crack addicts that dot the alleyways of Hollywood. He could live and breathe without some kind of fear breathing on the back of his neck. But he doesn't think much of what's happening. He's not like Joe. It's just the way things go sometimes.

*   *   *

The next day. Tommy wakes up under a bridge. He wipes the dirt off the side of his face. Bleary eyed, he stands up. Nothing ever seemed as beautiful as the sun high in the sky with the hot L.A. heat. He feels his heart pounding and his bones crack. Nothing so wonderful as the dirt under his feet and the mattress beside him that he'd fallen off of during the late night or early dawn.

He wonders if he could fall into it like he'd done so many times at home when love and freedom had been a sealed box under his bed. He thinks about that box and wonders if it's still there, lying peacefully in the darkness. Probably they'd been searched through, dumped out for some clue of where he was, he thinks.

They wouldn't find much. Inside are just a few photos of friends and family, a few ticket stubs and a blue wig he'd bought in Providence. If they ever thought to find him there, it'd be a needle in a haystack. There were so many street punks hopping trains and doing dope that one more would never get their attention. He'd hitched, so there was no money trail to his location.

Tommy checks his pockets and finds a small bag of coke and some money. He is alone under the bridge, so there is no one to party with, no one to take out for breakfast. No one. Joe had gone to one of his 'places' to keep rich junkies company and hadn't invited him for some reason, though the reason might've been compassionate. No reason to put the stuff right in his face, now. The back of his throat itches and Tommy smells blood in his nostrils. Carefully he takes the drugs and tucks them away in his sleeping bag. There was no sense in being caught with drugs. With any luck, he'd sell it today, or find it when the mood was a bit lighter.

But the darkness under the bridge has scattered into a thousand sun beams and Tommy feels alive like nothing else. He stows the cash in his wallet and finds Stephanie's phone number and address.

Why the hell hadn't he called, he thinks, but the answers were written in his dirty hands. For a novelty he was worth something, but full time he'd just be a cheap irritation. And it had been late. Tommy tells himself he'd seal his anxieties away and call sometime in the evening.

But it is not evening now and though he isn't hungry, he finds himself walking along the sidewalk to the subway and wherever that would take him, he'd go.

He is about half way there before he pukes his stomach out on that same sidewalk.

7.

The rest of the day seems to harden and at the same time dilute that moment. He gets to the subway, takes off his now off-white T-shirt and pulls a new one out from his bag. For pants he already has on a pair of ripped jeans that are supposed to be dirty, and on his face is a thin sneer. It's not so much that he sticks-out as that he simply assumes an individualistic pose and doesn't need anything from anybody.

Tommy had come a long way and he isn't about to be trapped. Never again, is what he thinks. He was born to be free. He feels a kinship with the other kids he sees on the street. Dirty faced and begging, while not perfect, was better than his last occupation as a scared, near-suicidal teenager in high school. Everybody on the street knew it and while he didn't go out of his way to approach his comrades on this rung of society, he didn't avoid them either. Something in his eye told them he was doing his own thing and didn't have time to be bothered.

But there were times that he'd given into the camaraderie of those living without walls, really work at communicating with them, but more than often than not these days he felt he was just being given the runaround. Just some rich drug-dealer slumming it with the dirtbags he pretended to be like before retreating back to whatever safety net he had. He knows he helped them, even just with breakfast, but they never comprehended that the only safety he had was the rooftops and alleyways of wherever public transportation could bring him. Tommy never mentioned it. He had no idea what they thought about Joe.

Sometimes someone would pull out a joint. Tommy didn't smoke regularly. A lot of the time the result of partaking was him wandering the city, stoned out of his mind. Maybe they have better pot here, he thinks, because he used to smoke joint after joint back home, but it wasn't like that now. Getting stoned made him feel like an alien.

He doesn't see anyone on the subway and as he sits, he considers his options. He thinks about going to a truck stop he knows which has showers and that's how his thoughts came around to Stephanie again.

Stephanie, Stephanie, Stephanie.

The name wasn't something that filled him with warmth. He guesses that she reminds him of Gina. There was something about her that made him think of home, though not the one he'd left. She promised something like life. A new home, a new host of responsibilities, commitments and relations.

If things got serious she would probably bring him along to her graduation, talk him into moving to the Midwest where they'd be closer to her family and finally wrap him in cellophane so that he could die of suffocation.

Tommy stood up briefly to crack his back. The feeling of nausea hit him like being on a merry-go-round for too long.

He would be tucked in a coffin perfectly like a doll that never left its box. Tommy doesn't even know if she's from the Midwest or when her graduation is, but he knows how these things go. Like a scared lost puppy, he was being trained better than Gina could've ever hoped for.

Everyone was involved, he think bitterly. Kind old ladies smiled at him on the streets while depositing a quarter in his cup and waited for a grateful, thank you. Police officers gave him hard looks till he straightened up his posture.

Everyone wanted you to be something respectable even if that meant years of attention and nagging to get you there. In the end, you'd just be another suit with a slick haircut and an eye for future investments as you turn your attention to training the next generation.

It was all useless to think about it, he thinks. He had only been with Stephanie for a night and that was that. She certainly didn't know of her complicity in this societal conspiracy. She just wanted to have fun! So, it was stupid to think about it, but that's just the way he thought. He wasn't apologizing for it. He remembered the man in the coffee shop and wonders if he, too, is falling into madness.

There's something to be said about manipulating trusting women for free sex and showers though, he thinks. Tommy concludes that he could probably do anything he wanted with Stephanie and still remain himself, but what that was, he couldn't quite say.

Tommy doesn't know what he wants to feel, but he thinks maybe it has something to do with waking up under a bridge, free and healthy and ready to take on the world. Maybe he could still feel that way with Stephanie, he thinks. Maybe not.

Confident, feeling like he's really figured it all out, he throws up again and gets ready to run out of the train at the next stop.

8.

Tommy spends the next few hours somewhere in South L.A. There is a park nearby, but Tommy can't face the rest of the druggies there. There is a perception of an alpha in the drug world and for a while now Tommy feels he's been it. On some days, the other kids in the park would approach him with their own custies, looking for a little blow, humble and forthright with their requests.

No one feels bad when a king fell, he thinks. At the train station, he quickly changes into another new shirt and then finds himself wandering around the neighborhood.

This is not a good situation for any homeless person of any age, race, or stature. He has to find a place to hide, but Zeke's house is too far away and the park is filled with people who'd love to take advantage of his state.

They could be kindly gents and ladies about it. He debates this to himself. After all, a lot of them shared his lifestyle and like Tommy said, sometimes they were good company, but he doesn't trust other drug dealers. Joe had always dealt with them before, sort of as a network of contacts to associate with, but more times than not the entire row of them were cycled out of society with places to go and places to stay locked up in. As for the other homeless who served as camouflage for Tommy's trade, they really couldn't be counted on.

By this time Tommy can't think of anything nicer than Steph-anie's breasts but he knows that showing up like this would just scare her. Keep your lady happy, Tommy thinks. He has a plan. Walking through an alley, he skillfully jumps over a fence into the backyard of an abandoned house.

He doesn't know the former owners of the house and he'd yet to see anyone else staying there, but he uses it as a last resort. Just a place to change clothes, throw a gallon of water over his body and from there walk to the park. He doesn't have a gallon of water inside him or out now, but if luck would have him, he'll stay out of jail and anyone's way until the sickness passes.

*   *   *

The next few hours were spent in unbearable agony. He sits down, he throws up. He stands up, he throws up. Finally, he falls face first into the dirt and squirms like a worm until his body cramps and his entire frame is bunched up on the ground.

He feels hot all over. He feels cold all over. He pukes and he pukes and he pukes.

The sun in the sky keeps its steady beat of radiation on his body, but eventually it too begins to set. Tommy is covered in sweat as well as vomit. Approximately two hours later he man-ages to get into a sitting position. This is ridiculous, this is too much. He decides to go to Zeke's house and maybe get a line or something to calm it down, but he can't stand up right and when he tries to walk he finds himself staggering against the wall of the house. He decides to stay. He decides to tough it out, but the decision really isn't his.

His fear of being arrested takes over. He stays behind the house and watches the darkness grow. To say that he sleeps would be a kindness, because all he does is moan and roll on the ground now covered with dried up puke. Tomorrow, he thinks. He'll call Stephanie, go to her house, make extraordinary love to her in the shower, then pass out. He hopes he'll still be alive in the morning.

*   *   *

Dreams. And after dreams, nightmares. Images of Kurt looking sad with his back to a mirror. Images of Zeke shaking his head above him and patting his arm. Images of his father with hands clasped behind his back. He was saying something, thinks Tommy, but he can't hear anything because a grinding guitar was pinned into his head. "Don't come back," he thinks he saw the words superimpose from his father's open mouth and he weeps, but then he thinks he sees Stephanie, then Gina, then his mother all watching him with tears in their eyes.

"I won't," Tommy thinks he says. "I won't do this again…" He wants to apologize, but can only retch some more, whether on himself or just in his dreams, he can't say. He reaches out and the only person left is Kurt Cobain and it's Kurt that takes his hand lightly in his.

"Are you sure you don't want another shot?" he asks softly, then dreams start to fade and he wakes up with the images of his father, of Kurt, turning into the newly-shaved head of Zeke.

"Mwahhh," he says intelligently.

"I said, do you want another shot? It gets better, I swear!"

Zeke asks. The scenery behind Zeke is blurry, but Tommy feels dirt next to his stomach. He is ass flat on his belly, staring into Zeke's eyes who is bent down next to his head.

"No, I…"

"Just want a place to lay down in, huh?" Zeke shakes his head sadly. "You east coast boys are no fun, really, you're all a bunch of posers." Tommy tries to get up, then lays his cheek against the ground.

"It's all the same with me. Lucky, I was around. You were making all sorts of a scene. Do you remember, do you remember me sticking my neck out for you? Shit, if I hadn't been around, you would've been dumped in the park for the cops to find. Shit. If I hadn't been around you might be dead for all I know."

Tommy groans.

"C'mon, we'll get you to the house, I'll doctor something up for you. You'll be fine."

Zeke grabs his shoulder and unceremoniously picks him up off the ground. Tommy doesn't know, Tommy doesn't care. Zeke pulls him to the front yard, then shoves him in a car. Mike is in the driver's seat.

"What have we got here?" he asks as Zeke pushes the seat back to get in himself.

"Nothin'. Just another victim of the drug age," he says it almost under his breath. "Good thing I was there. Good thing."

Tommy doesn't know what to say so he remains silent as Mike drives the both of them through the desert landscape to the front of Zeke's door. He slumps in the backseat, checking his pockets and generally tried to compose himself. What had happened?

What had happened was that some of the squatters in the area had found him in the back of their house. How Zeke had found himself with them remained a mystery, but, apparently, he had saved him from getting mugged.

"Fuckers would've stripped you alive," Zeke tells him from the kitchen of his house, mixing up some kind of gin mix. "You have no idea what I had to do to make them leave you alone."

Turns out Tommy was right, there was no love from the drug park, he wonders vaguely what he had done to all those scum buckets, but it was probably just how he acted to make them think he was an asshole and didn't give a shit. More than likely they saw this all as a big joke.

Because Tommy never joked. Because Tommy never had fun. He is a loner of the first degree and now he's receiving the hatred he deserves.

"There now," Zeke thrusts the drink in his hands. "So maybe another shot wasn't the best idea, here's this, just take it, take it and go to sleep you motherfucker. Sisi is gonna kill me over this, I swear." Outside his vision, Tommy hears the now robed Sisi in the hall.

"Is he going to be ok?"

"He'll be fine, honey, just go back. I'll be there… like I said, just don't cause any trouble, we don't want any trouble." Tommy nods or thinks he does. He takes the glass, downs it, then forces himself onto his side.

"Great, golden, you'll be fine. There's a little tar in there. I think it should help. Just get out as soon as you wake up. You. Remember. Leave when you wake up." Tommy gurgles something, then closes his eyes.

"You got till tomorrow morning, son, don't let me see you here at noon."

*   *   *

Kurt is sitting with his legs against his chest by a giant mirror while Tommy sits smoking a cigarette.

"Whatdaya gonna do man?" he asks. "I gotta tell you, you screwed up big time, you can't afford this, these are your only friends, once they figure you've gone wrong, there's no coming back from that."

Tommy sits up and blows a smoke ring.

"Really?" he says. He lets the sarcasm weigh heavily in the words.

"What are you talking about? This isn't your place, this isn't your home!"

"This is my home," Tommy gestured with his cigarette towards Kurt. "What are you doing here, why the fuck can't you stay away for once! This is my house. Everything I see is mine! This house, this street, this city!"

"You're going to regret that, this isn't your place, what the fuck have I been teaching you?"

"Fuck it, fuck you! This is my house," Tommy stands up. "This is my house!"

Kurt just looks at him silently. Tommy turns around, finding a bottle on the couch, he picks it up.

"And I can go anywhere I want and not you or anyone is gonna stop me! Nobody here has the guts to stop me! Do you hear? This is my house!" Tommy closes his eyes as he turns back to the rock star. He opens them and sees a pit bull leaping at his chest. He screams.

"Aaah, get it away! Oh shit oh shit!"

"Y'see? Y'see? This is what that got you, this is what you got." Kurt pulls the dog from above so the creature was inches from his face, straining towards Tommy.

"This is what you get fool! You want more? Keep talkin'! Keep talkin' that ghetto shit, we'll see what happens! This ain't your place, son! You got it all wrong!" Tommy screams some more, but he wakes up with a dry throat. Daylight was shooting through the blinds. He picks up his bag and takes off.

*   *   *

"I just think, fuck this, I'm going to be true to my own code. My punk ethos, do you know what I mean?" Tommy nods towards Stephanie who's wearing sunglasses as she drives her four-door sedan into her parking lot, talking up a storm. It'd been a long morning.

First thing out of Zeke's house he heads for the beach. Upon getting there he tears off all his clothes and jumps into the sea. The smell of salt clings to his hair as he washes out the day-old vomit from his chest and crotch.

When he gets back to shore, he pulls his other pair of pants, clean, over his hips and another shirt from the plastic bag in his pack. No need for her to see anything, he thinks, then he dries on the beach, no blanket, no headrest, just let the sand and shells stick to his body. He lies there for quite a long time.

When he is finished with his nap, he looks around for a payphone and gets out the phone number from his sleeping bag along with the little bag of coke. As he calls he draws out a line on top of the receiver and snorts it when Stephanie comes onto the line.

He thought she wouldn't recognize him, but she doesn't say anything except, "I'll be there" and then hangs up. He has a girlfriend, he thinks and the idea makes Tommy cringe. He doesn't know how he feels about it, but there is the necessity of getting the hell off the street until the sickness passes at least. He doesn't know what had been in that gin, but his stomach rolls underneath him. He does another line off the cardboard of his sign then lies back down. An eternity passed.

When she picks him up she is all smiles and kisses. Tommy deals with it like one would an overly excited aunt, gets into the car and they are away. That's about the time the talking started.

"I want to build something, I want to give something back and once it's done, I'm out. Take the money. Split to put my toes in the sand, like you, y'know, just get away from all the drama and bullshit…"

Tommy remembers his real girlfriend back in Boston. One night they had been making out outside her house and she had pulled back with a mysterious smile.

"Wait," she said, then got out of the car. Tommy waited.

He watched her poke around the windows of her parent's house, then open one of them on the basement level. He gulped. She jumped inside. For what seemed like forever he waited, then suddenly she was at the driver's side of her boat of a car.

"Try this," she forced a bottle to his lips. It tasted like candy.

"Huh," he said. Gina smiled and took one herself. She got back into the car and drew his candy lips into an embrace. There was a long pause as the music got to the end of the tape.

"Do you think we'll be forever?" she asked.

"Of course, baby, of course," they kissed again under a full moon on a summer night. Nobody could equal that, thinks Tommy, but somehow things were changing by necessity.

"I'm not into the games and the drama and the crowd," they say together. "I only want you." Tommy looks up at the gorgeous face smiling at him in the winter heat.

"You too, babe," he said. "You too."

*   *   *

"What do you want from me?"

Tommy looks up to see a man in his late twenties standing over him and his pack and sign.

"Excuse me?" asks Tommy.

"What do you expect me to give you money? You, with this torn shirt and pants? Did you dress yourself that way just to fool guys like me? Well, it's not working, not this time, pal!"

"Just a little change," Tommy looks at the ground as he spoke.

"Well, forget it, it's not working. I got your number bub." The man looks up, straightens his shirt and walks off. Tommy doesn't care. He'd made about twenty dollars off the streets today. Not a bad haul, he thinks. And less dangerous.

Things at the club aren't going well. As soon as Joe and he arrive, the big man shows up and ushers Joe inside. When he comes back, he cut the bills he'd gotten for the coke and gave half to Tommy.

"He says it's getting hot out here," Joe says. "He said he'll take what we got off our hands, but not to come back for a month." Joe shakes his head. "He gave us about half of what we'd make, but it was right there and he can burn us if he'd like…"

Tommy stands up, pockets the money and pulls out a cigarette, a Marlboro. He senses he won't be having one of those for a while.

"Well, that's it," Joe continues. 'I'm gonna try to get a run for some of the people I know, if you want, you can come with." Tommy smiles. He lights the cigarette and puts his hand on Joe's shoulder.

"Looks like we got off tonight," Joe mumbles. Tommy continues to smile. "So, I guess we could get drunk?"

It is more than a question. It's like Tommy is supposed to hate him for this turn of events, like he was going care about this after ignoring all the other reasons Tommy had for hating his soulless flesh-sack. Tommy slaps the kid gently on the cheek before bringing his arms around his own back and cracking his spine. Joe has some serious confidence issues, thinks Tommy. He must not have had many friends. By now, time and drugs had washed Joe innocent in Tommy's eyes.

They cut over to the rail station and get some tickets, then take a train south to the Japanese district right by the jail. That's where Joe liked to go. The bartender didn't care and the people, while Japanese, were kind to them if unskilled in English. Sometimes a street urchin could make it in this world.

*   *   *

Back in the streets, Tommy feels tired. It's been 10 days since leaving Zeke's and while he still feels strange, the sickness is gone. He has not been back. In fact, he hasn't been anywhere except downtown to beg and Stephanie's to fuck. The passerby had been right. He had a clean set of clothes in his bag.

Stephanie never questioned him on what he did all day and that was good because it would've led to a lot of awkward moments on Tommy's part, but Stephanie's mind was all over the place. He would be surprised if the thought of a life outside herself would ever occur to her.

She was crazy, like really. She'd shown him the pills and despite her doctor's advice she smoked and drank. Secretly, she confided to Tommy that she was on the verge of a break through and pretty soon she'd be off the pills and the therapy. Tommy doesn't care one way or the other. It's nice to fuck.

Generally, though, he feels like he really likes her. He tells himself this. At times she is animated and simply nuts. At other times she's quiet and let Tommy hold her hand while they watch TV. The Simpsons were more fun to watch when any moment you could find yourself in a kiss. Never in a million years did Tommy think he'd find another lover so perfect for him and those thoughts kept him warm at night. He had left one girl only to find a real woman. Did it really have to be so hard to be happy?

He debates with himself on the morality of his situation. It hadn't been fair to leave Gina. Or his friends. They at least deserved an explanation. And it wasn't right to leave his parents. They never did anything wrong. Tommy closes his eyes and runs his fingers through his hair. His sister probably doesn't even remember him, he thinks and that burst of negativity gives him the strength to take out his package of rolling tobacco and keep him from crying. He kept the tobacco around because it was hard to justify Marlboros to his well-wishing patrons. It's really fucked up.

Sometimes he'd find himself just standing there in the middle of the sidewalk, lost in some subconscious universe. As hard as he tries to ignore these increasingly common incidents, they continue to happen. Just randomly at any time, day or night. When these moments of subliminal introspection did occur he had to walk to the nearest building and sit down. Start giving himself a silent talking to. He hoped it wasn't too obvious to those looking on.

Is he becoming a crazy person? Is he losing himself? Would all the dreams of freedom and an eternal summer steel themselves and turn to ash against these guilty, subconscious attacks? Maybe a rock star could help him, he thinks to himself sarcastically, then curses himself anyway. He is going crazy. He's become the crazy bum who has a musician in his head.

Someone drops some change in front of him and he just

wants to scream. He grabs the cash and picks up his things. It was almost noon, but he doesn't care. He'd call Stephanie and fuck his cares away.

As he turns down a street to intercept the subway, he hears a voice call his assumed name.

"Tommy!"

He turns around to see a small Mexican woman in her twenties. She is smiling and in one hand holds a purse while waving the other in the air.

"Oh, it is so good to see you," she says as her waving hand opens in embrace. "You're looking good!" Tommy closes his eyes and begins thinking it couldn't be that bad.

"I was just going to an interview, I mean I did go, now I'm going home, are you well? We haven't seen you, you know, you don't have to ask us to come by. It's just as well. Boy, it's so good to see you!"

Tommy smiles a little and holds onto Sisi's hand as he shifts his pack.

"Come by anytime," she says. "I gotta go but take care of yourself. OK, bye!" She hugs him again and smiles before walking away, but looks back and waves. Tommy waves back and watches her go. He hadn't said a word.

PART III

1.

Tommy tucks his free hand under his head and lets a column of smoke expel from his lungs. Life is good. Stephanie is in the shower and he's alone with his own thoughts and the twisted sheets of their bed.

Despite their prior worries, Stephanie's room-mate is rarely home during the day and sleeps soundly at night. Stephanie is skipping a class, but Tommy doesn't care. He is living the punk dream; money for nothing and your chicks for free. He smiles. He hates the song, but everything has its place.

He puffs on his cigarette. Still rich from the last big sale, he's smoking Marlboros and after those run out he could smoke Stephanie's. Maybe being an old hippie-bum full of platitudes for girls like Stephanie wouldn't be such a bad thing, he thinks. It could be an aspiration. It certainly wouldn't be that bad if these girls let him live with them. At least two out of five days.

But there were moral complications to the idea. Freedom is a hard thing to give up. Just face the long summer into eternity, thinks Tommy. The truth is that Tommy doesn't want to be anything he isn't already. Being inside is like being molded. Just like college, just like jail. Conforming to society isn't one of Tommy's strong points.

The shower stops and Tommy tries to come up with something to say that isn't too derogatory towards his lover. He hears the phone ring. Stephanie curses then the ringing stops.

She bursts into the room, hair and body wrapped in towels with the phone pressing into her ear. She is talking fast.

"Yes, yeah, I know, but I slept in, no big deal," she's saying. "Yes, I know it's important. I'll talk with her… yeah, believe me. We're on the same page. OK, yeah, bye." She dives into bed, letting the towels fall as she rolls into Tommy's prostrate body.

"Are you gonna clean up?"

"Hmm, yeah," says Tommy, kissing the top of her head. He leans away from Stephanie's clean smelling body and stubs out his cigarette. He starts to get up to shower and leave.

"Wait," says Stephanie suddenly, pulling him back down. "I want to share something with you." Tommy groans inwardly. Probably something about how much she loved him and life. And the universe. Oh, it was fine when he went on, he thinks, but it doesn't sound right coming out of her. Is poser the right word?

"No, no. It's not that," she says as if she knows exactly what he wants to say. "This." She turns quickly and digs into the condom drawer. "This," she says again and pulls out a small vial of white powder. Tommy cocks his head in interest. What is this?

"This was supposed to be Ecstasy," Stephanie says as she pops the top. "But it's not, it's something else…. Heroin." She almost whispers it. "Wanna be a rock star?"

Tommy could've punched her, but instead he takes the vial, pours it on the back of his hand and sniffs it all in one go. After that, he gets up to vomit. Tommy knows it's coming. He makes it to the bathroom and pukes all over the floor then flushes his face in water. Well, it wasn't normalcy. He turns on the shower before he remembers Stephanie. He is a step from the door before she says something that really blows his mind. Doesn't even know if it's real or not.

"How you doing babe?" she calls. "That'll teach you not to use too much. Just with me." Tommy wonders if she knew about his addiction, or was just sore she didn't get any, then gets into the shower. It was now official. They are a junkie couple.

*   *   *

If there is one thing Tommy would change; it's be the heat. It's all encompassing, not completely unbearable, but the sun is always in the sky and those on the ground get the brunt of its wrath. Meanwhile, millionaires sit in air conditioned offices. He sits on the beach front and contemplates this. He'd been doing a lot of contemplating lately.

After leaving Stephanie's house with a head full of dope and her off to school, he'd instinctively found his way to the Pacific. He and Stephanie were having a fight. It was a strange, passive aggressive thing as they sized each other up. Beginning to see the real person behind the charade. True to form, as a moody Gen Xer, Tommy left and came here. It was so peaceful and free. Like he'd thought before, he could really grow old here.

The beachfront isn't deserted, but from the way he sits you could say he is alone. Arab is probably around someplace. He wears a clean pair of jeans, slashed at the knee, his Nirvana T-shirt, also freshly laundered and his pack lies at his side.

Stephanie had kissed him at the doorway of their home and then gotten into her car to get to the rest of her classes. Before he left, he sopped up all the puke from the bathroom, then threw the paper towels into the dumpster. She hadn't done any of the drugs and he guesses that it was all some sort of test to see if he had a taste for it already. He isn't sure if he'd passed or not. Maybe he's just being delusional, he thinks.

She had been very cryptic and strange. He'd just stood there, letting her wipe his face with a towel and cover his body with kisses. So much wrong with this. With the world. With them, he thinks. Why is he so happy now? The waves crash in and the waves fall back.

He knows what it is. He enjoys being molded. Enjoys being told what to do. The fight was a shadow box. His worlds are colliding. The amount of their desire was turning to jealousy and while he'd never even given her a line of blow, she'd known all along he was into all that and had hidden it from her. Now she was trying to surround all of that world and turn it into something about them. Making him her fuckin' tool, he thinks bitterly and breathes heavily.

But he likes it. It's all too fuckin' unreal, but he knows it's true. He likes it and he wouldn't think of ever letting go, but... what was he going to do? He doesn't know, but something about the sound of the tide puts him back together. Like he always knew it would.

The light plays out over the water and Tommy, seized by some kind of panicky energy, gets up and runs into the waves. As he gets deeper, he's slowed down by the water sloshing between his legs, but he keeps going. Jumping and leaping, he makes it through the tide till he is up to his shoulders. Then he takes a quick deep breath, closes his eyes and sinks to his knees. A chill grips his body that has nothing to do with the temperature. It wracks his form as he flails his limbs. He pushes upward and finds himself much deeper than before.

For a moment, he's one with fear, but he starts to swim towards what he hopes is the shore. Soon the ground is under his feet again and he beaches himself, wet clothes and all, back on land. He finds his pack and collapses onto his belly. He closes his eyes and breathes hard. What a good life, he thinks, then promptly falls asleep.

Tommy wakes up in a strange trance. He is laying on cold sand and the moon is out. He stands up and wipes the dirt off his still damp clothes. He almost jumps as he notices the sunset on his left. Somewhere in his sleep he must've rolled 180 degrees, he thinks, ignoring the obvious fact that the sun was supposed to set on the ocean, not the land, then jumps again at the strange spectacle this daily phenomenon has made. It hadn't always been background to him, he used to be really awed by the sunsets here, but this is totally different.

It's green, with white rockets streaming through it from the center. A very peculiar trait, he thinks and would've sat down to study it more, but he then notices a concert stage between himself and this spectacle and a few men and women on top of it. They're putting speakers into positions with such finality that he wonders if they are constructing Stonehenge. Although odd, he doesn't give it much thought, that is to say, he feels his thoughts being directed away from thinking anything unusual was taking place.

"The concert will commence in 30 minutes," he hears a voice say, far more clear and less booming that what an ordinary microphone produces. He frowns and looks about for some source, but there was nothing to imply such a voice. Just himself and the sunset, the waves and the stage.

The stage workers move in perfect silence. Unwrapping wires and heaving speakers to and fro. Now the lights from the stage seem to glow and some normalcy comes over the sun. Like a thief had stolen its splendor and left it still beautiful, still pure, but a little more ordinary than it was before.

He watches the stage and is surprised to see the workers dismantling. Sensing something off, Tommy walks over towards it and after a few steps he stands at the front end of the structure. Strange how things seem different, he whispers. A man on the stage puts a hand to his ear and silently words a question. It must be the surf, Tommy thinks, carrying the smallest tones such distances across the sand.

"What's going on here!" he almost shouts. The words are like a howling siren.

"Show's done," says the man, wrapping a wire. "Weren't ready."

"Why?"

"Don't know. Drugs or something."

"Oh." Tommy tries to look defeated. He'd never felt so let

down and this upset. And the sea, the surf.

"Don't worry, chap," says the man. "They'll be another one. We'll be ready."

"Ok," says Tommy, almost whispering then ambles along the shore. The stars were showing which was odd. He gets his pack and leaves thinking he'll climb a porch to a roof. It feels like something to do...

As he stands on the rooftop of some family's home, he channels the light of a million stars rushing through him until he eventually falls asleep. Happy in a way.

He dreams about stars for the rest of the night and then quite unexpectedly, the next morning, finds himself making the bus trip to Zeke's house before he's even rubbed the sleep from his eyes.

It isn't that he's being drawn by the promise of drugs. He wants to be away from the drugs and the streets. His rambling relationship. Everything. He wants be somewhere where it just didn't matter who he was, or what he felt and just relax. Somehow this equated to his drug dealer's home. Tommy had by this time forgotten the confrontation between himself and an imaginary rock star and only remembered Sisi's invitation.

While he doesn't have any intention to use again, he also doesn't see the danger of being in its immediate proximity. The incident with Stephanie had been just a small bump in the road towards his abstinence of a drug that made no real difference except on the TV where superstars find themselves in expensive clinics. To him, it was a thing in the past and not worth reckoning with again. He wonders if everyone ended up thinking this way. It's all behind me.

So, his drive to go to Zeke's house was the same as before he even considered getting into dope. He figures he'll just watch a few movies and maybe bum a pack of smokes from his supplier, catch up on the schemes of the day and generally put in some alone time. The thing was that while Zeke was a junkie, he doesn't flaunt his drug use and he despises pot. It seems to be a safe zone and that's all Tommy wants. He just wants to exist. He rubs his forehead.

Goddamn, why must he have this song in his head?

He deals with the chords of Lithium for the next hour and gets off a small walk from the Zeke and Sisi's abode.

"The continuous right to live does not depend on a piece of paper!"

Tommy hears the voices before he gets to the front door.

"Get out of here, you bum!"

Mike walks out onto the doorstep, shakes himself off from whatever psychic energy he's just exited and walks directly past Tommy without saying a word.

"Tommy!" shouts Zeke from the far end of the room. "My good friend, come in, come in." Tommy steps across the room smiling, a little embarrassed.

"We haven't seen you for a little bit. What's happening? Heard you saw Sisi downtown? You aren't still doing that bum thing, are you? You don't have to do that, we're business partners!" Zeke is drunk.

Still smiling, Tommy pushes himself into a chair while Zeke saunters across the floor of his one-story domain. "What was that all about?" Tommy asks.

"Oh, nothing, bad vibes, sometimes you just need to let go. Where've you been? I saw your little friend. He bought all the blow off me then just took off, what's with that?"

"Oh." Joe had apparently taken that road job. Tommy hadn't been informed.

"Whatever, whatever, take a seat!" Tommy is already sitting.

"Well, you'll have some lunch at least... Sisi! Make an extra sandwich for Tommy here!"

Tommy hears a crash from the kitchen.

"Tommy?!" Sisi's voice pierces the darkness in the room. The big window up front is covered in venetian blinds. "Oh sure." Another crash.

Tommy looks around. The room is in disarray. A pillow in the corner covered with feathers, a wooden chair carelessly left on its side. There seemed to be a new layer of paint on the walls, but it was just in pieces covering partial blocks. Tommy looks to see what graffiti was covered up.

"You guys have a fight or something?" he asks, trying to appear nonchalant.

"Nah, just a little redecorating. Listen, do you want something? I got a little dope, maybe we could set you up? It's a different clientele, but you're experienced. You can handle it."

"No, no, no," Sisi walks into the room. "Tommy doesn't do that stuff anymore. Right Tommy? No more dope!" Tommy looks at each of their faces before giving a shrug.

"I guess she's right," he says, also nonchalantly. "Y'know, Zeke, the real dough here is ecstasy..."

"No, no, no," Sisi hands him a sandwich. "All the drugs. Nothing for you! That is..." and here her voice lowers along with her stare.

"That is... unless you want to?"

Zeke looks hard at him all of a sudden. Sisi spreads her hands, also staring. Big, brown eyes bore into Tommy's skull. Zeke speaks.

"Yeah, Tommy... you into that?" Suddenly uncomfortable, Tommy shrugs again, trying to keep up his smile. But he remains silent. Zeke picks up the trail end of the subject.

"Well, if you do, I guess I could make some moves, y'know, a lot of that is made right here in the city, we could make some money..."

"No, no, Tommy doesn't want that! Do you Tommy? Tell me. What do you want?"

Under her gaze, Tommy feels stupid, far from the bravado he'd felt moments ago. He feels like a child and in that living room he understands why he'd run. He stands up suddenly but then just searches his pockets for smokes.

"I don't know, man," he mumbles. "This... situation..." He doesn't want to mention Stephanie now, he thinks

"There's a lot of change comin' about, y'know, and I think it might be a good idea, y'know, for the people and the money..." he says instead. Sisi looks at him hard now, then raises her hands as if exasperated.

"It looks like we have a raver, Zeke," she puts her arms by her side. "I'm gonna do some laundry."

"Yeah, I'll clean up in here, honey," says Zeke. He makes a half-hearted effort to pick up a pillow, misses, then manages to get it with his fingers on the down-turn. "We'll stop talking about it if you'd like."

"No, no. You play your games. Tommy, listen, don't get too into that stuff. It rots the brain." Tommy lights a cigarette. Zeke gives him a sour look.

"Well, we'll talk about it some other time," he mumbles. The room seems to swell then contract. Tommy smokes his cigarette. Reluctantly, Zeke reached into his pocket and pulls out a bag of weed.

"Want some?" he asks. Tommy nods then sort of sits back.

"Not too much."

"Why?" asks Zeke, "You got somewhere to be?"

"No, it's nothing like that. I just have a low tolerance." Zeke shakes his head.

"And you wanna be an ecstasy dealer? Man, you gotta reexamine your life." Tommy takes the insult, cigarette held out from his body, elbow on the chair's arm. There is nothing to say. Tommy wonders what the fuck to do. This visit isn't going as planned. He could've dealt with a dozen staring Mike's rather than this helpless limbo he's been sucked into.

"I have a little coke," Zeke admits. "Maybe I could front it to you? Give you something to earn with. It must be hell sitting outside like that. Yeah, yeah, that's what we'll do."

Tommy is surprised, but Zeke had been acting funny for the entire visit. They'd both been. He takes a drag off his Marlboro and nods.

"If that's what you wanna do."

"No problem," Zeke seems to be suddenly old, bones twisting under his skin as he stoops to pick up the chair. "I'll put it together for you. Teenths, right?" Tommy nods again.

"Yeah, that'll do it man. Thanks."

"No problem," says Zeke again and goes to the bathroom. Tommy smokes his cigarette alone in the room. Sisi is banging around in the basement. Well, he thinks, that's what he'll do.

2.

He stares at the sign. It seems so simple to him. Just stand on the side on the side of the building, sell the drugs, call up Stephanie and eat at her house, fuck and go to sleep. Shower in the morning. Maybe go by the park after that, size up what's going down. That incident at the vacant lot still haunts his thoughts. Paranoid, Tommy thinks. He proceeds forward and heads for the alley.

Tommy walks towards the darkest part of the alley he can find, right next to the dumpster. There are various black bags around. They hold napkins, bottles, whatever. He goes to the spot next to all of this then starts in surprise. The big man is puking by the wall.

"Hey kid," yells the big man. "You gotta towel?" Tommy puts down his pack, takes out an old shirt and hands it towards the distressed man. He stands there, watching the guy scrape vomit from his face.

"Thanks," he says.

For a moment, the two of them stand in their silhouettes. Tommy, clutching his bag with one hand, the big man washing sweat from his brow. They both seem to connect somehow. Like some strange, causal relationship and Tommy wonders how this guy had gotten into this position and whether he could follow in his footsteps. They are almost like father and son with all the variables that are brought into that equation, but Tommy doesn't want to go into any of that. Still, it's a strange thing.

"What are you doing here?"

Tommy shrugs, he could easily ask the same of the him. But the big man has a point. What is he doing here? The entire fabric of his universe seems to be held up by stage props and is barely balanced on the floor. What was it? It had seemed so simple, but now...

"I guess, I just wanted to sell some drugs," he says. It' a pitiful answer, but the big man nods as if he knew it all along. Like he didn't even need to ask the question.

"Alright," he says. "You stay here, I'll send them back to you." Tommy nods, pausing to throw his bag among the junk and garbage. The man gets up from his stooped over position and wipes his face again. He has on some kind of black shirt that appears to be silk, dress trousers and new, shiny shoes. Somehow, he'd avoided vomiting on any of them. Tommy wants to ask what he was so into that it had found him in an alley, puking his brains out, but he holds his tongue. It was probably the same dope cut ecstasy that Tommy tried.

"I'm glad you're here," says the big guy whose name Tommy doesn't even know. "We've been getting into problems inside and I wanna keep you out of it. It's real simple. People will tell me what they want, I'll walk away, then tell them you're in the alley. You want me to collect any money off them or anything?"

Tommy shakes his head. It isn't necessary.

"Alright," says the big man. "I'll be in touch."

The big guy leaves and Tommy is by himself willing away the time with thoughts of Zeke and his house. What was up with that? He wonders to himself as he passes the minutes, kicking the dumpster, hunkering down in his gray hooded sweatshirt. Just bored out of his mind. He wonders if he'd always felt like this, but by now, he doesn't even remember how he had started in this business. It was all a blur. Like a clouded, dusty movie that no one understood anymore. A spaghetti western, he thinks.

Slowly, but surely, the custies come. Tommy barely has to say a word. They come with money in hand and trembling fingers. Within an hour he sold half-a-gram. When Zeke hooks it up, he hooks it up.

The money made tonight is going to fund him for a week. Tommy wonders how much one of those silk shirts cost. He has a real itch to go inside and make himself at home. Eventually the night wears down and he finds himself with absolutely no drugs on him.

True to his nature, he picks up his pack and leaves the alley, not even bothering to say goodbye to the big guy. It's just one of those things. He finds a payphone, calls Stephanie. She is home, says she'll pick him up. Whistling, Tommy stands on a corner of Sunset Boulevard and waits.

*   *   *

Stephanie is in a mood tonight. Apparently, she missed a test and that is grinding on her. Tommy sits in the passenger seat while she maneuvers the car and curses. It isn't worth getting involved in, so he says nothing. Completely silent. She mumbles something about needing to buckle down and do the work, but he wonders if any of it is useful.

Stephanie is a smart girl, but she's a procrastinator and it pulls her down into these situations. She had a real chance at going to a private university, but she put off doing the work for a scholarship. Stupid.

Gina would never make that mistake, but then again, Tommy isn't with her. He is with Stephanie and he supposes from his attitude that he wants her to fail. Not really, just a little spark of resistance to blow a tire off her well-ordered life. Once she failed, he'd be right and they could go on with their life. Tommy starts when he realizes that he'd thought of it as "their life." It is puzzling the way his thoughts run. Besides the general craziness that his life had joined him with, now he was thinking in the royal tense! It wasn't even anything, he says to himself. As insignificant as a runny nose.

Stephanie talks on, she wants some coke, but has no connection. Tommy doesn't even care if it's a test or not. Like it or not, he'll probably continue to sell to the very students she studies with. Without her being the wiser. He doesn't have anything anymore, so, he stays quiet. Silently, he wishes drugs had never become involved with "their" relationship. When had that word become a part of his lexicon?

Eventually Stephanie wears herself down and when they get to the apartment, she rushes in without holding the door open. Tommy has to leap to catch it before it locks. It is a glass door with white letters that tells the viewer who to call if it was broken.

The rest of the night stays like that. While Tommy lays down,

Stephanie brushes her teeth. When she comes to bed, Tommy turns to kiss her, but she only gives him a peck and the lights turn off when she claps. What a weird girl, thinks Tommy. She rolls over to her side and pretends to sleep. Tommy stares at the ceiling. After a while, he falls asleep.

While he slumbers, Stephanie gets up and goes to the bathroom, rubbing her nose. The door closes behind her and Tommy sleeps on.

When he wakes up, Stephanie is already in the kitchen. Her roommate had left for the day and Stephanie is making breakfast. She smiles as he wanders in. Tommy groggily itches at his stomach.

"Hey, sweetie," she says.

"Hey," he replies. The room is filled with the smell of pancakes and bacon. She was cheerful after what? Three hours of sleep?

"Do you have to do anything today?" she asks.

"Um, no, not much, you?"

"I'm going to class at twelve, but I'll be back in a few hours, why don't you sleep in?"

"I'm already up."

"Well, just clean up a little and I'll be back. Charlene shouldn't be here till tonight."

"Does it really matter if she sees me?"

"Well, I guess not, but I don't want it to look like you're living here. Just try to be small, ok?"

Tommy doesn't really know Charlene, Stephanie's roommate,

except that she is always busy. No morning revelries for her, she is out running. No afternoon nap, she's in school, or internship, or work. Stephanie's parents paid for her part of the rent. Charlene barely seemed to talk to her's. Tommy thinks that if you put Stephanie and Charlene together you'd have the perfect woman. With Charlene's ass. Tommy smiles at this mental infidelity.

"Ok, I'll try," he says outwardly.

"Great, let's have some breakfast." For about ten minutes the room is filled with chewing. Cleaning her plate, Stephanie wipes her mouth then takes Tommy's and her plates, back to the sink.

"Be back soon," she says. Tommy watches her grab her bag and then open the door. He wonders if he should take her hand and kiss her sweetly.

"Bye!" she says as she leaves. Tommy smiles and voices silently that he'd miss her.

Then it was just him at the apartment.

He felt like the king of a castle.

Going into the living room, Tommy switches on the TV to watch the news. Most of it he doesn't understand, so he idly changes the channels. So much for the park, he thinks. He tries to relax. The park. It was just a bunch of hippies. Nothing worth getting upset over. At this point, if Tommy had his way, he'd be on this couch day in and day out.

It's a different from his former digs, but it's still free and as real as a bench on the sidewalk. At least, that's how he feels. He just appreciates it all the more, he thinks, fuck all that paranoia about being molded. Perhaps he was growing up. After about fifteen minutes, he gets bored and goes into the bedroom to grab his pack and sort it out.

The bag is filled with the oddest things. A sleeping bag, of course and some clothes, but also rolls of film that he'd bought when he felt like a tourist. They mostly showed the front of clubs that were closed for the day and the Pacific. There were also pamphlets of Jesus-talk that missionaries give out. The city seemed full of those do-gooders and they were all over Tommy like flies to shit. He puts the papers carefully into their own pile.

He separates clothes, clean and dirty, and finds a tape by Black Flag that Stephanie had given him. It's all unwound now, but he also finds a pencil and he rewinds the cassette with it. A serious task.

His tape-player is filled with sand, in fact, the whole bag is coated. He uses an old brick outside the apartment to keep the door propped and shakes the pack out. Back inside, he gets ready to do laundry.

The fact of the matter is that he is really a grateful house head. What had he been doing outside? He guesses that it was the climate, which made everything seem warm and cozy. Still, he remembers how he'd spent some chilly nights wondering when, or if, he'd ever find a home. On those nights when the moon wasn't full and the music wasn't jumping, the harsh realities of his choices had made him change his tune about what freedom meant.

And now here he is. Tommy doesn't judge himself for this. He just isn't all hardcore. So, he'd become a home-bunny, so what? At least he hasn't worn out his welcome, Tommy thinks.

Tommy wonders if he was somehow wrong to feel safe, but he lets the thought go as he fills the laundry machine. It'd all be OK.

While the laundry does its thing, he makes the bed and then lies on top of it. What a life, he thinks, then wonders if it would always be that way, or if he'd just become some old bum. Stephanie will take care of me, he thinks and that brought a smile on his face, almost a laugh. He doesn't know why, but he feels good and he feels like Kurt would approve.

*   *   *

Sometime during the last half hour of his clothes and sheets in the dryer, he falls asleep, then wakes up rejuvenated. What a day! In a couple of hours Stephanie would be home, he thinks. He smiles dreamily as he goes down to the laundry room. When he gets there, he finds Kurt Cobain sitting on the washer.

"Hi," Tommy says, trying to be confident.

"Hey," says Kurt.

"What are you doing here?"

"Oh, I don't know. Reminiscing."

"Well, it's got nothing with me."

"Why are you angry?"

"No, well… it's good to see you, I guess."

"Right, well, take care," Kurt dissolves and Tommy wakes up on Stephanie's bed, crying.

3.

It isn't that much longer before Stephanie comes home. Tommy washes the dishes. Just stands there. Feet motionless. He ruminates about the problem. It's obvious that Kurt isn't going away and he's expanding somehow to moments when Tommy thinks he's awake! He regrets even hearing of that band.

Time stands still there, standing in front of the sink, drifting idly from one dish to one more and Tommy gets lost in the repetition.

By the time Stephanie gets home he's back on the couch. Just socks, jeans, a T-shirt. Watching infomercials for no reason at all. He keeps his face steady, quietly studying what lay in front of him without questioning it to any degree. Simply lost in the moment with time running past like it always does. Staying for no reason without perceiving the future, without analyzing the past. It was sort of like jail, just slowly trying to keep it together for when the bars opened and socialization became necessary. Thank god, that had never happened.

Stephanie walks in, slams the door and walks past the couch towards the bathroom. Tommy puts the TV on mute and stands up to stretch. A moment later, Stephanie emerges holding her head.

"I'm dying," she says. Tommy turns to look at her.

"I'm dying and there's nothing you can do about it. You might as well leave."

Tommy stands perplexed, then angrily walks over to her. Stephanie had her head down, a few tears trickling down her face. Tommy grabs her in a rough embrace.

"I just don't know what to do anymore," she says, settling her body into Tommy's. "I feel so alone, I can't… I'm getting sick…"

"It's alright," Tommy says, rubbing her back. "It happens to everyone."

"Not you!"

"What? I'm constantly putting myself down. I'm confused and overwhelmed. Don't you understand? We're in this together!"

She cries a minute, then begins to stroke his neck. Soon they were kissing and retire to the bedroom. What Tommy doesn't know is as soon as he slept, Stephanie got up to go to the bathroom. Rubbing her nose again, she slips back into bed and falls asleep. It was late evening. When Tommy wakes up the next day, she's gone.

*   *   *

What maybe no one knows about Tommy is that he is secretly a massive tourist. Scraping together some dollars from the roll he kept in a pocket inside his pack, he moves by public transportation to the Art Museum.

Any trip like this made Tommy glad to be alive. There is something very punk rock about going to a museum without any requirement to. If there is such a thing as punk rock, it is about breaking boundaries. Going beyond what society expected. Most people would picture him in jail, he thinks again. Not the L.A. Museum of Art.

The concept of money has gradually radiated its way to Tommy's brain. Often, he has none. Then he's on the street, just asking for change. Avoiding the cops. But suddenly, at any moment it seems to him, he could be flush with drugs and cash and he walked like a boss into the depths of this world. He ponders to himself whether he has just fallen into a trap made by old men. For the love of money, he thinks.

The Los Angeles Museum was a sight to see. Big and sprawling, it was a far cry from the narrow streets of Boston, constantly refolding into more houses, more tiny driveways to public housing ruins. L.A. looks now. L.A. looks fresh. It is an epiphany of newness.

The scenery astounds Tommy, to the point where he doesn't feel he can even enter. He almost walks to a corner and takes the time to look for cardboard, but two cops roll by in their car and that was that. He just doesn't feel right, but somehow his clean clothes give him the courage. I'm not some street rat, he thinks. Just another respectable college aged kid here for the culture. He hangs onto the idea as long as he can.

The inside is quite formidable, too. Walking around, rubbernecking, he moves in the general direction of the check-in desk. On the walls are huge paintings by people he'd never meet from places he'd never be, born maybe centuries ago. Was that right? Were these ancient cave drawings, or just some kid in Soho? Tommy doesn't know and doesn't care. The beauty of the place makes him feel like a fly in the zapper. Completely electrified.

Eventually he checks in, gets a bracelet for his wrist and wanders off to the right. All around him are admiring individuals, sometimes in groups or just two by two. Somewhere, someone talks about this painting or that, but Tommy moves away from them. This was his world. He finds himself standing far behind the jostling crowds.

Museums are like streets, he thinks, staring at an abstract. Mostly it was just people going, here and there, but there were loads of strolling passer-bys, just idling away their days. He thinks he recognizes some faces from downtown. Maybe, but not likely. He assures himself that they don't recognize him. And what if they did? They'd probably approve.

"Breathtaking, isn't it?" A voice behind him speaks in a level tone. Tommy stands silent. Just another snob from Belaire, he thinks, telling it to his latest date.

"Excuse me," says the voice and a figure steps out beside him. "I don't mean to be rude, but it's so refreshing to see the youth admire art such as this. He started with murals, y'know, his work has disappeared now, but it's so moving to see the vitality of what's left." Tommy looks on cautiously.

"I'm Jim," says the figure, a dark haired, wide faced man who looks not a day over 22.

"Are you talking to me?" asks Tommy.

"If you don't mind. You seemed alone and I loathe to see a lonely face. I'll stop if it bothers you." Tommy considers this.

"No, I don't," he says finally, "My name is Tommy." The figure, the man, smiles.

"Tommy, graced I'm sure."

So, they walk around the museum, Jim pointing out this and that while Tommy nods and interjects questions that occur to him. He feels a bit in a daze, like he is walking on air and at the same time an emotion of oppression like his arms is about to sink to the floor grips him. It feels like a real contradiction of feelings and Tommy's stomach gurgles as they pass each artist's work.

It's late in the afternoon by the time they leave and then Tommy finds himself at the Tar Pits, Jim still nattering away about his opinions on art, politics, music.

"What do you think of punk rock?" Tommy asks quietly. Jim could've been talking about Beethoven for all Tommy knows. He feels confused, but like he must keep asking questions.

"Oh, I've been listening to punk rock all my life," says Jim. You wouldn't know it to look at him. Jim has on dress pants, a black belt and some kind of T-shirt made from a fabric that Tommy wasn't familiar with. It was blue.

"Do you like it?" Tommy persists.

"What?" Jim seemed flummoxed as though Tommy had broken a train of thought. "I love it. In fact, there's a show I was going to see tonight. Would you like to come?" Tommy stays silent a moment then nods.

"Yes, I'd like that."

"I got it, don't worry about money. This should be a good show. They're from Mexico, I think, and…"

Tommy kind of tunes him out from there. Jim hasn't really

answered his question. Tommy guesses that he wants as long as an explanation as that of Rembrandt, or Picasso. Tommy had heard so many things, in and out of dreams, from cassette tape lyrics, articles in "Rolling Stone", anecdotes from fellow travelers, in trendy cafes and street alleys. He'd traveled to the state of California, following something indescribable to be here in L.A. Seething with rage against the system, he was now finally being invited to see a show.

He feels out of place and weird though. Wasn't this what he'd been waiting for, to be a part of something bigger than himself? He knows one thing; he can't go barging in, he has to be invited. It didn't make any sense, but that's how he felt and this time, maybe, just this time he'd find what he was looking for. Not confused with drugs, or sex, or dreams, or hallucinations, just a pure state of music and togetherness that would supersede this mundane world of tourists' traps and beach sands. He didn't even know he had felt this way before now.

But now he realized it was something that he'd always dreamed of. He'd have traveled the world to find it and for some reason now was the time. It was time to reinvent himself. He remembered being drunk at some house near Berklee College of Music and all the kids jumping about some punk rock about to be played, but it hadn't happened. The cops had been called. In fact, the closest he'd gotten to live punk rock, what he'd anticipated as punk rock was in a church basement, but it had turned too melodic. He'd wanted Neil Young in his newest reincarnation and they'd served him "Harvest Moon." No one had enjoyed the show.

"Sure, we'll get dinner and then drive to the show. Right this way, Tommy?"

There was nothing special about Jim's car. It was black, warm and as Tommy enters it, he's very aware of how dangerous it is to get into a stranger's car. He'd hitched across the country, but it's funny how things from childhood crop up. They take the highway and Tommy notices that they are traveling east, away from the ocean and into the desert.

After some twists and turns, mostly at high speeds, Jim parks the car and they get out. He mentions something about the best burritos in town, that he lives nearby and usually walks. They sat down at the restaurant and Tommy took it all in as he ate the very authentic taco. One of three on his plate.

"Tell me about yourself, Tommy," Jim questions. Tommy chews, then sips through a straw some kind of rice milk drink.

"Nothing much," he says. "I'm from the East Coast. I decided it wasn't for me. I've been living here for a few months now."

"And why did you come?"

Tommy sips again and swallows. "I was looking for myself," he concludes. Jim nods and bites into his own burrito.

"A lot of times we find what we're looking for in our own backyard."

"Sure," says Tommy.

"But for some, travel is the only answer," Jim continues. "I'm like you. I grew up in Indiana. I came here for work, but I feel everything about it was fated."

"Yeah."

"Every day I surprise myself."

"Good."

"I want you to know. I almost didn't speak to you, but something compelled me."

"It's alright."

"Good," Jim sips his own glass of water. He had paid for the meal. "So, let's go!"

Tommy isn't particularly surprised when he observes they're riding in Hollywood. Jim smiles a lot as they both listen to some punk band on a cassette tape.

"The band we're seeing is much better," says Jim as he looks for parking. "I'm not sure where they are from in Mexico exactly, but I've heard a lot of buzz, I guess they moved here like us. I mean, this is the center of punk rock now."

"Have they lived here for long?"

"No, but they got lucky and have been bolstered by a lot of gigs around town. This is the first I've ever seen them, but their album is great. I have it at home."

Jim pulls into a parking lot by a club that looks familiar. Again, Tommy isn't surprised to find that it is the same club he works beside. It was that kind of night. Jim mutters something about trendy one night stand bars, then gets out of the car. Tommy follows only partially obstructed by the fact that he wore a seatbelt.

4.

"Let's go!" says Jim again and they plod quickly but purposefully to the front doors. Tommy was momentarily dazzled by the inside. Red walls with a lighted stage. Three people on it, drums, bass and guitar. Apparently just tuning up. No one stops them at the door, but Jim nods at someone on Tommy's left and they walk through unencumbered. In the corners, there are a couple booths and Jim leads Tommy to one.

"I can't tell you how excited I am for you to be here," says Jim. "They're really a rebirth of the whole movement!"

Tommy nods, aching to take something of the enthusiasm from his host, but only finding that cold gray he'd lived with for so long. That he had no words to describe. His former joy has been crushed. A server of some sort, a pale white girl with a black Mohawk, approaches. Jim talks to her while Tommy sits on his hands. Why had everything turned out to be just another four walls? Tommy is confused by his turn of emotion, but he sank down into its familiarity.

"I hope you don't mind," Jim says. "But I ordered for you." The girl walks away, hips ticking like a metronome. Tommy wonders what Stephanie is doing and whether she'd understand his roller coaster of thoughts and moods.

Tommy has certainly stayed nights away from his blonde

sweetheart in the past, but not when she was so upset. He feels like he should be with her, so, he resolves to call her and get picked up at their normal spot down the street. That is if she answered. She might be pretty angry after last night's emotional explosion. There's sometimes, he deliberates, that a man had to be there for his girl. He almost made an excuse to leave when suddenly the lights dim and the first discorded noise pours from the stage.

The bar girl emerges from the now fast filling crowd of punked out twenty-somethings with leather jackets and hair. They applaud as the drum beat suddenly kicks up and the girl drops a glass of coke with rum onto the table.

"This is it," says Jim and gives the girl a couple of dollars which she accepts without a word. "You're going to love this!" And the music starts.

Pretty soon the room was a multitude of colliding bodies up and down, side to side, mashing and moshing through each other, like balls on a billiard table. The music plays loud and heavy as the young Mexican screams into the microphone. Tommy looks over to Jim who is smiling profusely and then slowly, steadily, Tommy gets to his feet.

"I…"

He doesn't get to finish his sentence as he walks into a tall, white mustached individual who pushes him between a black guy and another Mexican who are obviously loving life.

They're shoving each other in the ping pong ring as Tommy tries to stay balanced. They rock back and forth. Tommy pushes back and soon he's comfortably in motion, jostling his way to the stage and back again. Vaguely, in his periphery vision he sees Jim get up and put his drink down, lifting his arms as some sort of brotherhood gesture and then he was in it too. Their lines of vision were obstructed, but Tommy feels this force of infinite connection. Maybe he'd just been nervous? He rocks, he rolls, but he doesn't fall. The band finishes their first song.

Then something begins to happen. As Tommy pants for breath, the walls seemed to shudder, then close in. It was the same floor space, but everyone looks taller.

The bass starts at some sort of rumble, shaking the foundations of the club. As Tommy looks around in bewilderment, he thinks he sees Jim except now his face is dead white and when he smiles Tommy could see that his incisors are long and pointed. Like a vampire.

All around him people are transforming too. Some bearded fellows begin to act like wolves, the mid-riffed woman in the center of the crowd seems to have blood pouring out of her hollowed out eye sockets.

Tommy dares to take a look at the stage and sees flashing lights and rows of smoking craters. When he sees the lead singer's face, all that he could make out of the singer's head is some short brown hair over which a perfect mask of an angry Kurt Cobain sits. The image meets Tommy's trembling gaze. The song moves faster and Tommy feels himself being let go into a multitude of monsters.

Some kind of lizard man smashes into his back and Tommy

falls face forward barely able to bring his hands down in front of him. Around him zombie hands ask him if he needs help as they shoot off the frames of skinny, rotting ghouls. Someone smiles as they pull him and he sees the reflections of damned souls all along their cheekbone.

"Thanks," he mumbles and tries to get back into the crowd, but no sooner is he up when reptilian hands wrap around his neck and he goes down on his knees again. This time he pulls himself up, but the lizard man keeps coming, smiling hooked teeth, dark, all black eyes and a deep throaty chuckle.

He comes at Tommy with two hands facing forward, but Tommy has had enough. He puts up one hand and winds up with the other. His fist plasters the thing mostly on the chin and Tommy feels a sting in his knuckles. It feels good.

It feels so good he can't stop. In moments, he was on the crocodile, smashing him with both fists as the lizard quakes and rolls up into a fetal position. Tommy leaps to his feet and starts belting him with heavy booted kicks along the chest, neck and head. Then someone is screaming and it takes Tommy a second to realize the noise is coming from his tortured lungs.

"No!" Arms wrap around Tommy's torso and pull him into the air. The walls are back in their slots, just mirror-like apparitions of their former chaotic states. The people look like people again. Some young guy with long brown hair like Tommy's was lying motionless on the floor. Some of the dancers group around him in a circle. The music was just a few distracted chords as the band finish their second attempt at ecstasy.

"We don't do this!" a voice hisses behind him and Tommy is barely able to turn his head. He's in the grip of a very strong man and it takes him a moment to realize who it is. It is Jim.

"We gotta go!"

Jim pulls Tommy, now lifeless, out of the club. Tommy thinks he sees the big guy behind the bar. His face is thoughtful. Tommy just focuses on breathing. The night was finally early after all.

Back at the car Jim is cursing as he unlocks his door. Tommy stands behind him.

"Sorry," says Tommy to Jim who finally gets the door open.

"It's alright," he growls. "Well, you need a place to stay, you can bunk at my house."

"Um," Tommy says. "I kind of have a place." A bell chimes somewhere. Tommy wonders why.

"Well, I can bring you to it! I don't think anyone's going to report on you, but it's late. Wait, who are you staying with?"

"My girl," Tommy speaks the words cautiously then hears the chime again. He shudders.

"She might be kind of mad at me, but I can call her. I don't think she wants me to bring anyone over…" He stops, then turns to look Jim in the eye. "Maybe I'll take you up on the offer." The bell chimes a third time and suddenly Tommy thinks he hears the sound of crickets.

"Yeah?" ask Jim. "If you're sure."

"Yeah, I'm sure."

"Well, hop in."

They drive through the city streets, street lamps whizzing by while the radio plays a crackling embrace of future and love and hate. Advertisements for the masses. Music for the initiates and all the while Jim pounding out a bass beat on the steering wheel while Tommy's face is glued to the window.

Watching and catching glimpses of billboards, he sees people on the street on their night out, or just street people shuffling to and fro. The boy stares. The car stops at a light and he sees an old man standing at the corner, not sure if he can go on. Tommy sinks lower in his seat. He's nervous, for some reason and he sets his mind to answer why. Trying to block out indecision and doubt, he realizes he's having trouble with his stomach. Eventually they get to a side street and Jim parks the car.

"I guess this is it," he says. "You sure you want to come up?"

"Why wouldn't I?" Tommy asks, stretching silently as he unbuckles his belt.

"Well, y'know, going to someone's place…"

"I don't get it."

"Well, it's not something for one's reputation."

"I don't have one."

"Well, you should know… I'm gay and I'm attracted to you."

"Oh," Tommy feels drunk, like a slow tortoise in a race not meant for him. "Well, if you're not going to do anything…"

"Oh, I am." Tommy ponders this.

"No," he said. "Seriously you'd do that?'

"Anything's possible."

"Well, maybe I should go…"

"Yeah, I figured," Jim unbuckles his belt and reaches a hand to Tommy's shoulder. "I don't want to ruin this. I know you have a girlfriend…"

"Don't worry," says Tommy courteously. "I'm glad I spent this night with you."

"So, I guess you're going to get moving on." Tommy opens the door, ignoring the beeping the car makes. Jim gets out on his side.

"I'll be fine," say both Jim and Tommy at the same time. They cross the front of the car and meet halfway. Tommy embraces the older man, breathing in the smell of cologne.

"It's been great," he says, then lets go. Somewhere a gong sounds and Tommy is down the road while Jim watches. Tommy is looking for a payphone, but he can't find one. Finally, he spots a double-decker deli and climbs quietly onto the roof. No one ever looks up. He falls asleep in a half embracing fetal position under the moon while the music plays on.

*   *   *

Tommy wakes up late in the night feeling something along his thigh. He kicks reflexively and his foot meets something in the dark. There is sudden a muted curse. Tommy feels soft cushions under his frame and immediately sits up. Somewhere a light clicks on and Tommy realizes he is in the living room of a small apartment. He hears some water running and he is gripped by fear. How has he come to be here? In his head, little bells of alarm start ringing.

"Jeez, Tommy," says a voice that sounded male.

"What is this?" Tommy asks. "Where am I? Who are you?"

The water stops running and a man in boxer shorts, no shirt

and a cloth pressed against one eye steps out.

"Shit, Tommy. It's me, Jim."

"What am I doing here?"

"Well, you wanted to come up, just to sleep, but y'know, I warned you…."

Tommy is already on his feet grabbing his pack. He moves fluidly towards the door.

"You could have been more firm!" He hears Jim behind him as he rushes down the stairs.

"Whatever," he calls back and then he's outside.

"We're not all like that," says Kurt, sitting on a garbage can. Tommy doesn't care, he finds a bus stop and promptly falls asleep.

5.

Five days later, Tommy finds himself at Zeke's house. The last week had been wasted. Walking around town, visiting different neighborhoods. Moving slowly around the area. The shower at the truck stop had been the most memorable moment. He feels as though he is in a cloud and the only effort he makes is to sit around storefronts with his pack and his cardboards sign proclaiming that he is homeless. He uses the money to buy cigarettes and food.

He doesn't bother calling Stephanie, doesn't bother selling drugs, doesn't bother to take pictures, write in journals, meet new people, visit landmarks. He does drink from a bottle of whiskey that someone gave him outside a liquor store. It was from a young woman, but he didn't pursue her. He still remembers the half quizzical expression on her face. Tommy just picked up his pack and moved on.

Somewhere along the way he decides to go to the park. He doesn't have any drugs to sell, so it was even more boring than usual. He just sits in the corner of the lot which really needs a make-over. Drinks and sleeps. When he wakes up, he sees a row of kids, homeless kids with tattoos and baseball hats wander in a line towards the street. He wants to sleep more so he gets up and heads to Zeke's. He ought to have some place to lie down for his partner.

Zeke isn't home but the door is open and Tommy hears some singing coming from inside. It's early evening, so Zeke is most likely still at a bar with Mike keeping the day interesting. The song is a sweet up-and-down melody, probably never recorded, maybe a folk song from wherever Sisi was from. Tommy barges into the house, throwing his pack onto the floor. The singing stops.

"Who's there?" Sisi's voice comes from the kitchen.

"Tommy."

"Oh, Tommy! Hold on a moment!" Tommy sits on the couch and waits. Soon Sisi comes out smiling.

"Tommy! How good it is to see you? How have you been? Where have you been?"

"Oh, you know, around."

"Would you like some coffee? I love coffee at night or evening, isn't it? I was just making a pot. Would you like some? I can share."

Tommy holds up his bottle.

"How 'bout we share this?"

"Haha," Sisi laughs, "I'm not sure, give me a minute… Let me get you some cups, y'know Tommy, it's not very sanitary to drink from the same bottle."

"Right."

Soon Sisi is sitting on the couch. A cup of coffee, cream and whiskey sits in front of her.

"Y'know, Tommy," she says. "I don't know what to make of

you. You're always wearing those ripped jeans and doing something..." A hand flutters in front of her face after she takes a sip.

"God, this is strong. Y'know, Tommy, you've got to move. You could do better, not that I wouldn't miss you, but every time you're away I think, well, maybe he's got a job or maybe he's moved back home and then I see you on the streets and you're not moving at all or you're over here discussing some pipe dream with Zeke..." She takes another sip, Tommy wonders if she even knew the extent of Zeke's pipe dreams, but he smiles and takes another sip as well.

"I know, I shouldn't be making judgments and sure, I live pretty close to the ground, supporting Zeke with my job and I don't mind. I make my own choices to make for myself something I can live with... but Tommy, what are you doing here?"

Tommy looks at Sisi reflectively, then crosses his legs and puts down his glass.

"I came," he begins and he is unconsciously bowing forward as he speaks to the ground. "To learn something. Maybe it was just about myself, but I..." He looks up to see that Sisi has moved so close to him he could almost feel her breath on his cheek.

"I came," he begins again, but then he turns his face to hers.

In a moment, they are sharing a long kiss. It's perfect, outside of time. Nothing like Stephanie drunk, or after an argument with Gina. It's love, he thinks, then tries to readjust his terms. It's two people, he decides, who want to become one. He doesn't know what Sisi thinks of him. If he reminds her of some high school crush, or if she feels like Florence Nightingale looking over her flock of patients and finding just the perfect one to take care of forever. It's all unclear. For his part he just feels... he doesn't know how he feels.

The kiss lasts for about a minute, then without a word, Sisi picks up the glasses and the bottle then walks to the kitchen. Outside, Tommy hears the sound of a car pulling up. In the kitchen cleaning noises begin as Zeke charges in with a black tank top on and some kind of silver necklace with big chains attaching each loop. Mike follows behind him.

"Whoa, ho, Tommy!" he shouts. "How do you do?"

Tommy laughs under his breath. He knows the truth in his bones: if Zeke had wandered in a few moments ago, Tommy would've been murdered. Tommy begins to look at this situation differently. Zeke isn't some big-time drug dealer, he has connections, sure, but he's small potatoes and he blows it all on beer and gas for his car, as well as enough heroin to keep him from feeling sick. Sisi's the one with the paycheck, she keeps him on a leash. That makes Tommy happy. Zeke isn't as free as he's made out to be.

"Tommy!" Zeke says again and falls onto the couch. "Where have you been? We've been talking, me and Mike and we're thinking of a road trip! What do you say? Are you in?"

"Haha," laughs Tommy. "You really think I'd be a benefit?"

"Look at the big words! No, Tommy, you'd be great. Think about it, we could get high in a graveyard in New Orleans! Complete mission." Tommy smiles and shrugs. He files away that Zeke would be out of town.

"No," he says. "I'm pretty much L.A. now."

"Doing what? Bumming for change? Do you need anything? You've been such a friend that I'd give you some just to get you thinking. It'd be part of your share of the trip..."

"Just put it on my tab, huh?" asks Tommy. He already owes a bill for his last escapade. He keeps it in a small plastic bottle in the bottom of his pack which he now reaches for.

"Well, I guess I should be up front," Tommy says. "I'm not leaving L.A. There's some things I have to take care of, if you know what I mean."

Zeke's face darkens for a moment and Tommy could see the lines around his eyes and forehead. But it quickly melts away.

"Well, if that's the way it's gonna be..." he suddenly reaches into his pocket. Tommy's breath catches in his throat as Zeke pulls out a small black box. Thinking he was about to be stabbed, Tommy makes his last prayer for his kid sister back home. It wasn't her fault he was so messed up, she didn't deserve this... but Zeke opens the box to display a syringe.

"We can still have fun here, can't we Tommy?"

There was a small crash from the kitchen and for a split-second Tommy thinks he was about to be saved, then the singing starts again. There was no getting out of it.

"Sure," he says. "We can still have fun."

The smile on Zeke's face was the last thing he remembered of his third shot.

PART IV

1.

The third shot is generally known as the last shot before you're addicted. It's all downhill from here. The rich become poor, the arrogant needy. Everyone knows that, at least they did in the small town where Tommy comes from. Even with his suburban background, Tommy knows a little something about drugs. In fact, as he searches his memory somewhere between waves of refreshing coolness followed by heat, he realizes he knows little else. Everything is stronger on the West coast, he adds to himself.

Tommy reflects that his whole life would be different if he'd just stayed away from drugs. Maybe he could've started hopping trains, or beach combed the entire coastline. He looks young enough to make more than enough money begging to take care of himself. Instead, life had just sucker punched him. The drugs had just made life easy. He could be in San Francisco with all the other muddle-headed, acid popping individuals, but then what? He was a drug dealer, he realizes and maybe he'd never be anything more.

At that moment, his heart seizes and he is back on wave after wave of euphoria. Dimly in the background of his retinas he sees Zeke passed out on the other end of the couch. At some point Sisi had taken away the syringes and cleaned up after their little dope party. Mike is in the chair staring sullenly at the ground.

If things had been different, he thinks, he'd probably just hang out with Arab, get a job at some kabob cart or coffee shop. He hasn't even tried. He's always so busy, or so he feels and this is where it left him. He watches himself breathing heavily with drugs in his veins and a pulsating light in the center of his vision. He can hear whispering around him and he thinks of Kurt, but no angel or devil visits him this night. This high is all his and his alone.

He resolves to never do it again, but he is already beginning to itch along his shins and calves. He claws at himself and the light turns from white to blue. He feels himself jerk awake, then finds in his dreams a little girl playing with blocks and then awake again to see the TV scrambled and Mike gone from his chair. He thinks he hears movement elsewhere in the house and a woman's voice moaning.

Could it? He tries to figure out the situation, but there really is no time to deliberate as he feels his body ascend into space again. High above everything he wonders how much Sisi took and what she took; to complete herself and in what way. He wonders if Zeke even cares. The face of his drug dealer, dark and foreboding, stays with Tommy. He realizes with a chill that he may be present for a hot-blooded murder scene.

Or maybe not. Maybe he is just hallucinating the whole thing. He catches a glimpse of Zeke's prostrate form once more before he too passes out.

If the night has terrors, it doesn't affect the heroin addicts of the world. At least not when they're high. Later vivid dreams of the things they do to continue on will wrack them on sleepless nights, but for now Tommy is safe. He sleeps, dreamless and completely alone.

Somewhere a mother says a prayer for her only son and somewhere law officials trade photos of the missing child. Because that's what Tommy is.

There are many and many more follow. That doesn't bother the detectives working on the case. It is well known that his is a situation that has many scores of refugees. No home. No parents. And the cancer spread outward to affect every person connected with the file. Just one case in a million. Some come back on their own; pregnant or scared, or mixed up on some drug, or people, or something. Sometimes it's for the best and they don't ever come back.

Sisi is peacefully asleep when Tommy awakes. Mike is back in the chair. Tommy neither knows nor cares what the drug head had been doing all night, but somewhere inside himself he knows he has to go.

It doesn't matter what plans Sisi has in mind for Tommy. Tommy couldn't move onto a new life, as much as he wants to. He begins to speculate on what it could be like. Pick up the pieces of his existence. Just hunker down and explain to somebody what he's gone through and what he wants. He didn't know what to say last night, but he knows now. His dreams. His passions. His life. Where it is and where it was and where he wants it to be.

The feeling of emptiness and loss fills his heart. But... one look at Zeke's sleeping body tells him to run and to run quickly. If he stays for even a minute more he'd be sidetracked again.

"Just one more shot?"

Tommy hears the words not yet spoken by his sleeping compadre. He doesn't know why, but the dread of that situation takes him by the throat and imagination steps in to fill in the gaps.

He'd probably end up driving with Zeke and Mike wherever it is they planned to go and then get whored out to the first gay porn magazine Zeke could find somewhere in that lonely South. Why not? All tied up and high as anything for a bunch of closeted Southerners. A lot of people do it, after all, and when the sun goes down, that's free hunting time! Tommy tries to tell himself that he's wrong. Zeke doesn't know, thinks Tommy as he begins trying to move his legs. Terrified by what one kiss can do.

If Tommy had gone to one of the youth centers that dotted the city's landscape instead of this drug den, maybe he might've found someone who cares. Someone that understands and the road back to redemption would be open. All the nice things in life. Job, home, friends. It's a sad state of affairs for a runaway to take stock of his life. He has to get off these drugs first, he thinks, and that singular thought brings him back to his feet. He has to get home.

He moves like a robot, but he gets to the door. He'll pay Zeke later, or not. He doesn't care. He moves with purpose. The light of day holds no warmth. He finds a bus stop, then a train stop, then another bus.

He walks to Stephanie's house in a trance.

Stephanie answers the door. First there is questioning, then anger, but soon bewilderment as Tommy pushes past her and makes his way to their bed. He hits the pillow.

Stephanie comes up behind him and strokes his head.

"There. There," she says, pushing the matted, sweaty hair from his face. "I gotta go, but I'll be back. Wow, you really got into something." Her nose twitches and she lets go, but Tommy stares at the wall with uncomprehending eyes. Stephanie walks to the bathroom, then back. Picks up her purse and leaves. Tommy is alone in the bedroom.

He hears sounds from the living room. Stephanie's roommate getting ready to leave, then she and the sounds she makes departing are gone. Hours go by before he can leave the bedroom and then it's to the bathroom to retch into the toilet. When he does, he feels nothing. No high, but no sickness. Soon he's back on his feet and thanks whatever deity that watches over street kids. He's missed the bullet.

It had been too long between usage for the shot to throw him out onto that other pile of statistics. He lucked out. His stomach turns again, but it's nothing like before. He wonders why.

It's like he's been cured and he proceeds to make breakfast for himself. He even laughs! Thoughts of home are out of his mind and he decides to go back to Zeke's and score some coke later on. He's up to it tonight. Maybe with this score he can find a room to rent.

My, what a crazy trip! Too crazy to believe, he thinks. Just gotta act like nothing happened. Maybe he'll luck out again. Deep inside he feels a longing that could be for Sisi, or just heroin. Once again he feels his stomach turn as he finishes the bowl of cereal, and he retreats to the bathroom to puke again. Nothing! Merrily, he finishes the soley biological necessity of getting rid of his insides, and gets back to the kitchen, happy as fuck. No one would understand, he thinks, no one that hasn't already shot up.

As he's wiping down the table and counter he hears the lock click and in comes Stephanie holding grocery bags and sunglasses over her eyes. She looks frazzled, a little unhealthy.

Tommy wonders what she'd been up to for the week, but there was no time to ask as she streams into the kitchen, placing the glasses over her forehead and opens the refrigerator door. For a long minute there was just the sound of food being packed into the freezer.

"Y'know, you really threw me," she says. Tommy is standing next to her by the sink. His stomach gurgles, but he keeps his eyes on her. She speaks without looking at him. "I thought you were gone, but I guess I knew you'd be back."

"Listen, I'm sorry…"

"I don't want to hear it. I just want to know how it's going to be." A brief sob comes out. "I'm just not in a place right now where I can have just an on-and-off relationship." She turns to look at Tommy. "I want to know this is real."

"Of course," says Tommy stepping over to her to rub her back. "I'm really a mess like I said, but I guess I want to know that too." She responds to his rubbing and pulls her head into his chest.

"So, will you?"

'I'm gonna try, I am. Listen, we can spend the rest of the day together."

"No, I mean yes, I mean, there's something I gotta tell you…"

"What?"

She breaks the hug and walks to the hall, then the bathroom. When she comes out she is holding an almost empty bag of white powder. Tommy knows what it is immediately.

"Where'd you get that?"

"Oh, from this guy. I think he wanted me to blow him, but I bought it. It was a lot of money, but I've been so stressed and I heard this helped…"

Tommy leans his stomach and chest into the sink, facing the wall with closed eyes.

"You should've tried Prozac," he mutters. He feels like he is going to cry.

"I've never shot it, I don't think I'm addicted, but… you need to take this away from me. I don't want to be a junkie, Tommy, I really don't!"

"I don't either!" he reaches out and takes the bag away from her then shoves it into his pocket. "Y'know, I'm into this too…"

"But you're so free! You can kick anything!"

"I know, but it's hard… I can't have it around me."

"I'm sorry, I'll take it back…"

"No, no, I'll take care of it." He moves to the front of the house and scrambles down the hallway to the outer door, walks outside and finds a drain. He tears the bag a little and pauses to lick his finger. Not bad. He brings it to his nose and snorts whatever powder he can get. He feels nothing, but that's probably because he's still high from the night before. Then he shoves the bag and the rest of his energy into the drain. It's done. No more. Tommy wipes his face and looks around for Kurt to applaud. Kurt is clean, if you believe the television.

He knows what he'd do for another shot, thinks Tommy but he doesn't appear. Whistling, Tommy makes his way back to Stephanie. He is in sync. He is ready for anything.

But Stephanie isn't. When he walks into the apartment, beige walls casting off the light of two lamps, he finds her crumpled up on the couch. He doesn't want to be too affectionate. Some things are more important than sex and what she'd done was a major breach of trust. Tommy doesn't consider his own actions. He walks behind the couch and put his hands onto Stephanie's head and strokes it. She pulls away. Maybe a head massage was over the limit.

"Just… I'll be ok, why don't you do the laundry or something. My roommate won't be home till late. There's food in the fridge. I don't think I can eat right now." There's a sudden grumble in Tommy's stomach. He feels the dope in his own system reaching out to the drugs in hers. Riding that high, he obeys her suggestion and goes through the chores in a slow-motion, a meandering process that mechanically moves him room to room.

He finds some quarters on the bedside table and packs everything into a hamper. Feeling the heat of his efforts, he realizes the bump has actually affected him. He's very high. Nothing special, he thinks, giggles and pictures a giraffe bending his head to get at some leaves close to the bark of the tree. All the blood has rushed to his head. He's high.

He wants to go to the zoo. He wants to take a shower and lie on the bed. He forces every part of his sweating body to finish knowing that when it's over he can finally rest and enjoy his predicament. Kurt isn't in the laundry room either.

He finishes putting the clothes and sheets into the washer then walks back to the apartment. Stephanie is now in the kitchen.

"Do you want a grilled cheese?" she asks him as he sat at the table. "I think my stomach can handle that." Outside the sun is beating down while a breeze rustles the palm trees.

"Sure," he isn't hungry, but he's riding a storm. Anything could happen in these charged up moments.

"Listen, I've got to get out of here. I have a class."

"Oh?"

"I'm sorry, but will you be here when I get back?"

"I'm right here."

"I know, but I want to know if you'll stay!"

"Absolutely."

"Don't you understand? I need you here!"

"I'm sorry, I know… I'll be here. I promise."

"Ok." She shoves a sandwich off of the frying pan, putting it on a plate, then grabs her own sandwich right off the stove top.

"Thanks sweetie," she says and Tommy senses a bit of sarcasm in the statement. "I'll be right back."

"I'll be here." Stephanie left. Again.

2.

As soon as she is gone, Tommy runs to the bathroom and retches. He feels the bite of grilled cheese move up and out of his throat and then just bile. Wiping his face, he soaks his hands and scrubs vigorously. No more of that, he thinks, then settles on the couch to watch TV. It's momentarily distracting.

He couldn't stop thinking about Sisi. About Zeke and Mike and even Joe. All players in his drugged up L.A. Was Sisi really screwing around?

There was something about Sisi that Tommy was electrified by. Something. Strength. From what she said, she was an independent woman. No cook and clean slave. That was what Tommy had envisioned her to be, but now he sees there's far more. Tommy closes his eyes and tastes the remaining powder in his nasal cavity.

She is just more, what's the word? More real than Stephanie? When it comes to Sisi, anything is possible. She might have a degree in sociology, or psychiatry, or social work. She might be an ancient spirit worshiped by an unknown tribe, or descended from witches, or just sane in an otherwise insane world. Tommy doesn't know. He has no business to know. Really though, he giggles, how had she ended up with Zeke?

Tommy's mind flashes back to high school where some of the

hottest, smartest girls had chosen scumbags over football stars. These couples had taken upon something of a caretaker-caretakee relationship. Nothing like him and Gina. Nothing like him and Stephanie. He grimaces as he's forced to turn the magnifying glass to his own life.

Stranded in introspection, he does nothing with his day. He lays on the couch and watches game shows. It was probably for the best. His body didn't feel quite right and he's coming down from a terrible elevation that is his state of mind. He's not getting sick, no, but he is worn out and feels like death. Tired. All he can do is sit, sigh and shit. Eventually he zoned out into a steady rhythm of changing channels and yawning.

He wonders about Sisi. Did she control the house and who lived in it? Tommy would like to move into a house, get a job, kiss Sisi all over... he admits this to himself, but from what he heard, or thought he'd heard, that dream doesn't correlate with the situation. She was, maybe, screwing everyone and controlling everything. Maybe the kiss hadn't meant a thing to her. Maybe he was destined to worship her, become a slave to her wishes.

Or maybe his entire theory wrong. Is it her who was in need of saving? Is Tommy, or maybe Mike her knight in shining armor? Perhaps Zeke had saved her from the streets, but the going was getting too much with him high or sick all the time and she's stuck, trapped with a psychopathic boyfriend and grasping at anyone to somehow get out.

Tommy isn't naïve. He'd seen plenty of hookers in Hollywood. Some had made passes at him and some were pretty hot, but Tommy had declined. Disease, he thought, that was all it came down to. For a moment, Tommy wrestles with his sexuality, but that passes too. He has no idea if Sisi is the trapper or the trapped, the conqueror or the conquest. Tommy thinks of Gina for a moment and wonders how she'd look at the entire situation. Probably not kindly.

While he's pondering these thoughts, the sun shines through the window and Tommy regrets his thinking and his actions. Stephanie is a great girl. She had saved him in a lot of ways. For once he'd found someone that was on the same track. He isn't being carted from work to school, he is just experiencing life. And Stephanie? She's so full of energy and compassion.

They'd hit a rough spot, but that's no reason to leave for greener pastures. He tries to imagine himself without her and he could, he knows that, but it hurt. It was if someone was taking out his rib. He thinks momentarily of Kurt Cobain and his claim that it was his stomach that was causing all the distress.

Like Kurt, he'd found someone and something he couldn't let go of, no matter how much he might want to and everyone thought it all was a song off of Nevermind for them. It was the story of his brief, free life. Tommy blinks back tears, then smears the ideas from his mind.

Tommy walks into the kitchen still feeling down, but stable. The room is small, about half a school bus. It holds some appliances, a small table in it with two chairs and a window with curtains. Some floral print. He opens up the fridge and finds a six-pack of beer with one missing. Without really thinking of whose they were, Tommy grabs one and twists off the top.

It is a beautiful day. He unlocks the door, leaving it partially open then climbs down to the first step by the sidewalk. He uses a newspaper to keep the door propped open in case someone had locked it. That happens sometimes. He lights a smoke and sits.

He wonders if he has ever really loved anyone. He loves his family, he thinks. He feels sure about that but he'd left them behind. He had loved Gina, he loves Stephanie, he thinks he is falling in love with Sisi, but what if he doesn't really love anyone? Everything he did seemed so crooked and off… he takes a deep drink from the beer.

It was like he was looking through a glass window at himself. He moves and talks and touches and feels each and every sensation, but it is like he isn't even there. It's like his body is a piece on a board that he is connected to, yet somehow, somewhere else. He wonders if everyone feels this way.

It's been a long time since he's had normal emotions. Is this part of growing up? He deliberates on this atop the steps, smoking and wondering if he'll ever be the same again.

On the outside of the house's parking lot, he watches a police car pull over a Porsche and a scene unfolds. The officer gets out of his car and walks to the side of the offending vehicle. After a few seconds he walks away, steers his cruiser around the Porsche then drives off. A moment later, the warned driver puts his auto into gear and peels it out onto the empty street. Lesson unlearned.

Tommy couldn't help but think that he'd received quite a few warnings himself. He throws his cigarette on the ground and takes his beer back into the house. The minutes tick by as he rambles around the house, waiting for Stephanie to come home. Eventually he ends up in the bedroom.

He lies on the bed feeling nauseous and stares at the ceiling. He can't rest at all. It's as if he's been placed in a pit of unending anxiety. His legs itch. Starting from his ankles to his thighs. He's in agony, but he has given up trying to scratch them. The beer seems to help.

While he feels jacked up, like a coffee buzz, he also can't move. He watches the lights play with the ceilings uneven paint job and hallucinates white, fluffy clouds underneath a light blue sky. Perhaps an acid flashback?

Tommy wracks his brain but can't come up with anything connecting heroin withdrawal and hallucinations. He'd stopped paying attention at some point in whatever class taught that kind of thing. He's pretty sure that any junkie would laugh at him for even thinking that the two can appear simultaneously. But there it is.

Anyway, loneliness and sensations of abandonment are on his mind. He doesn't understand how he could feel so high one moment and so low the next. The drugs are playing with his head, he figures, but it's hard to concentrate on this idea. Finally, he drags his eyes off the now swirling dragons that rule the ceiling and starts to stretch his toes while he gets a cigarette out and begins chain smoking. God damn, he thinks.

He feels just plain useless. He thinks about getting another beer. It's a funny thing to be so young and yet so very imprisoned.

Gradually, he comes to the realization that he isn't in his home town and there are plenty of places to go and experience. Zeke's, for instance. Or some alleyway with some other junkie. Skid Row was supposed to be full of it. He'd never been there, maybe he should?

But he just lies there, contemplating his situation, ignoring the chemical temptations of another trek across town and delves into self-pity. It's not a good scene, but at the very least he is being responsible, waiting to handle his domestic troubles rather that running away. It's like a first step, he thinks and like an old man he cracks the bones from his toes to his neck, still lying in bed.

He remembers about a two and a half months ago he'd been high off all the cocaine Joe and he had been selling. High as a kite and so much money. That had been one of the first sales. After that Zeke, or maybe Joe, pushed up the asking price and Tommy had learned what it meant to be truly homeless, actually begging for change just to buy cigarettes and food.

Tommy copped a couple fives and went into the old bodega, or whatever they call it on the West Coast by Santa Monica Pier, and scored a carton of cigarettes. When he got out he found that Joe had abandoned him. Fuckin' kid. Tommy wasn't really hurt. You go where the energy impels you to go and there's very little that can be done to stop it. So, he continued to walk along the beach till about dusk and planned to meet up with Joe at the club.

Despite his open-ended relationship with a schedule, Joe was quite on time when it came to selling drugs and the clubs were the best place to make money. Tommy thought of it like doing the neighborhood a pro bono favor. Just target the adults, keep the kids out of it, I mean, weed is harmless, but put cocaine habit on a fourteen-year-old girl? What would the parents think?

Just then a figure broke out against the sun. Somebody was moving towards him from the ocean waves and very quickly. Tommy puts up his defenses until he realized that it was a girl. Even so he was a bit scared. She looked homeless, which is a hard thing to pull off in LA, he thinks with all the grunge branded fashion taking over the country, but her appearance couldn't really be explained by anything else.

It confused Tommy, there seemed to be so much opportunity here, but Joe had alluded that girls had it a lot worse. At the time, Tommy thought he was espousing some anti-sexist philosophy. Now, looking at this girl, he realized there was only one thing any man would want from her.

"Hey, can I trade you a lighter for a couple cigarettes?" Tommy realized he was smoking. At first, he thought she meant she'd give him two cigarettes for a lighter and he took it out of his pocket.

"I need it back," he said quietly.

The girl quickly explained that she wanted cigarettes, not a lighter, which she'd trade for the smokes. Very confused, Tommy got out his pack, mumbling something about it being a gift, then remembered he had a carton of Marlboro Reds in this pack.

"Hold on," he said and took his pack off. There was another plus about being a drug dealer, he thought. You could help people in need, hell, maybe start up a healthy relationship towards redemption? He had the money and he could talk Joe into cutting her in. It was the right thing to do.

"Here," he handed her a pack and as he did so she began to cry.

"Thank you," she said between starts of air coming out of her mouth without control. She took the pack and walked away, still weeping. He didn't follow. He didn't know what to do. This was what he thought of just before falling asleep.

What's seen in dreams can be much more than they appear. A sudden movement, a strange sound, a shadowy face. Let it be known that the imagination can be the worst demon that has ever plagued mankind. And it grows. It grows with each retelling of a scary story and words learned from dictionaries take on a new meaning in the darkness surrounding thoughts. Ideas.

Tommy's thoughts have always seemed so clear, but what is seen is only an edited version of a text of colors and urges that so often affect the young. So, when Tommy wakes up, he is free of all his strengths and weaknesses and he is something other than Tommy.

He rubs the back of a woman he's taken to mate. She had returned sometime while the sun was up and fell asleep on her bed. She wakes with no sudden realization that dreams are false and reality is interrupting, but fully waking to a cloud in which the dream is real and waking up is mostly the conclusion of a plot line that she has imagined. They kiss and what happens as body meets body is incredible.

Her hand reaches around him, to the bedside, opens the

drawer and pulls out a condom.

"I think we'll be alright," she says as she rips the plastic cover-ing. Giggling, they separate enough to apply the prophylactic.

"I think so, too," says Tommy, his voice somehow deeper and grander than ever before. They kiss and the stars explode over them while they enjoy a togetherness that makes no sound.

Without even a whisper, they both decide they'll cut down on the heroin use. Maybe just one line every week? This new dream was here to stay.

Before he had even gotten to LA, Tommy and Joe walked a straight black line in the desert of California. A sign said it was Octipello.

"So, this is it?" Tommy asked.

"We'll get a ride to San Diego and then catch a bus to L.A. I've got some friends and I've got to check in with my client."

"Won't they be mad?"

"It's their risk and their loss. Plus, these kilos were a bonus. I'll give them half of it to make up for losing their stash."

"Can you do that?"

"Sure. This is grown up stuff. We're all players."

Tommy pondered this.

"She didn't really understand," said Joe suddenly.

"What? Your girlfriend?"

"Yeah, she was just a guitar player trying to make it big. I told her to come onto tour with me. She didn't even question that I was bringing her van to a mechanic to load up."

"What? And you just left her with it all?"

"It's all behind me… but yeah. She'll probably get off."

"You really move on."

"It's what I gotta do. You'll see. Everyone in LA is after something. It's not really a place for close relationships."

"So, did you?"

"Did I what?"

"Go on tour."

"Oh yeah, I knew a promoter in Miami. He got her a show. After that we just hit town by town, looking up open mics in free papers and just basically walking into bars. We'd stay in a town for a day or two, then move on."

"Sounds nice."

"It was. We had it made." They came up over the top of a rise in the desert where they could see a diner with a few trucks in its parking lot.

"There's our stop. Hopefully they'll get us to the train route."

"Right."

*   *   *

The next day Stephanie takes Tommy to school. It's a breezy day and all of creation seems to congregate in the square that the campus surrounded. There's loud music, people on bullhorns, people with signs. Some march in circles, some chant slogans. Good grief, thinks Tommy, all this for a tuition hike?

As someone who doesn't even want to go to school, the event seems like a ridiculous farce. Why pay to waste your life in some pseudo-reality? Sure, they'd made some contacts, made big plans, but then at the end of it they're just going to be snatched in different directions by whatever turn the economy made.

It's a sad memorial for Tommy, just a poor choice during a poor semester to show some sort of solidarity before they were destined to part ways.

Stephanie walks right into the crowd dragging Tommy in by the hand. All around them people are chanting and in the front, there was a guy on a megaphone. He is tall, shaved head and wearing a thick pair of black eyeglasses. He's wearing a pink tank top, beige shorts and open toed sandals.

"Stephanie!" he shouts away from the microphone. "You made it!" The crowd is now calming down as students sit down and take out packed lunches.

"And this is?"

"This is Tommy," says Stephanie. "My boyfriend." It kind of thrills Tommy to hear that.

"Oh, cool, where do you go to school Tommy?

Tommy feels suddenly very young, "Um."

"Tommy doesn't go to school," Stephanie supplies. "He's a free spirit."

"It doesn't mean I, uh," Tommy says slowly. "It doesn't mean I don't support all this."

"Great, Tommy, it's a real gift to see the generation come together. Has Stephanie told you what we're doing here?"

"Um."

"He knows," says Stephanie firmly. "It's to support low cost education."

"And a better deal for graduating students," says the as-of-yet unnamed protester. "Y'know, Tommy, it's simple. These bosses are trying to keep tuition rates high and that means less students and more loans. Then they'll use the money to build unsafe industry and put people to work in uneducated jobs. They'll try to say they are turning around the economy through those jobs, but in essence they'll be controlling the world because no one who's not already in the club will be educated enough to see what they're doing! It's a classic Nazi play, putting the power in the hands of the few while the working class mindlessly works away their best years. Capital and Labor."

Tommy's impressed. It was the most eloquently phrased bat-crazy statement he had heard in a while. He wants to talk more about it, how the revolution could be started by waking people up, but that's just his hippie side suddenly coming to bear. He puts on his best punk rock face. Stephanie laughs.

"You have to excuse Matthew," she says. "He gets a little carried away."

"I am…," says Matthew, staring Tommy right in the eye as Tommy nods and looks down. "Just espousing my own theories, but that doesn't mean I don't support the cause." He suddenly holds up the megaphone. "Free education!" he bellows and a few whoops and hollers respond.

"We got a good thing here," he says to Tommy. "I'm so happy you came."

"No problem," says Tommy as Stephanie laughs and pulls him back into the crowd. "See you later."

Matthew nods and pulls out the megaphone again to shout a few slogans. Tommy and Stephanie find a corner between two buildings and make out.

*   *   *

"So, I don't know," Tommy finishes. Sisi and Kurt look on

solemnly.

"You know what I have to say," says Kurt.

"I'm with him," says Sisi.

"I never want to hurt anyone," Kurt says.

"Yeah, but what if!"

"There is no what if, you're happy now, forget it."

"I can't help but think for myself!"

Kurt laughs.

"You never need to think for yourself. It's already laid out for you," he stops. "At least when, y'know, where love is concerned."

"Do you have doubts?"

"I'll take this one, Kurt," says Sisi. She turns to Tommy.

"Do you really want me? Just me, not all the rest of the glamour or glittz because you seem to have a great girl."

"But you don't even know about her!"

"That's right and I'm not talking."

"Always look out for the silent ones," says Kurt.

"So, what am I supposed to do?"

The sun suddenly glares its way through the glass.

"We aren't responsible for you," say Sisi and Kurt together.

*   *   *

Down on the street, Tommy whittles away while Stephanie is gone. He purposely wore one stained T-shirt and sat with his legs spread. Ass on the ground. A cup stands in front of him and he just waits. You couldn't get more aggressive than that without actually speaking to anyone. Which he did not.

Stephanie's parents had sent money, but honestly Tommy just

doesn't know what else to do. So, he sits and waits. He waits while people sneer or hold their noses and a few coins start piling up. He wonders if he should write up a sign. Something like "Have A Nice Day!' on it with a smiley face, but he is too lazy. Seriously, further on down the street he hears a boom box and he figures it has to be the break dancers doing their thing. How could he compete with that?

It's clear, he's an object of pure pity, no other explanation for why dollars and change kept coming in. The sun is beating down. He thinks about throwing up. All this excess and bilious over-load. It seems to be the correct response. The truth is that life had suddenly decided to wedgie him with these feelings, these desires, these thoughts and he didn't care, he really didn't care, care, care care, he didn't care at all.

*   *   *

The days go by the way they always will. Tommy doesn't sell any drugs, but he makes do with sniffing up crushed pills Stepha-nie supplies. Sometimes they mix a little tar that Stephanie man-aged to produce from some one or another. He's been housebro-ken, a willing addict of pharmaceuticals and she's even got him thinking school might be a good idea, too. He's lost something, he thinks, but if the world is round, it's inevitable that two opposite forces will meet. The past is only westward after all.

It's about noon when Tommy finds himself at a bus stop already inhabited by a completely different breed of the street kid he's become.

The kid is asleep. In his hand is an old metal can and around his neck is a sign that says 'I'm turning dreams into reality.' Pretty funny. Tommy just wants to use the bus

Being as quiet and unobtrusive as possible, Tommy leans against the outer wall of the shelter which is new, relative to the city of L.A.'s history. Tommy whistles to himself. The kid stirs.

Tommy thinks it's just a sleep murmur, like a comatose patient in a hospital, tossing, turning and talking in their sleep, but no. It was in a matter of seconds that the street kid went from asleep to fully awake.

He has hair close to his shoulders, a striped hat, striped socks, some kind of red swimsuit and a T-shirt, black without anything on it. He yawns.

After a little while, after both of them had stared ahead for a minute or so, the kid digs out a packet of Top from his shorts and coughs heavily.

"Hey man, do you got a light?"

Tommy looks over to see that the street kid had already rolled a thin looking cigarette. He pulls out a lighter and holds it out at arm's length. The kid takes it. He must be about thirty, but drugs do strange things to a person's face. His is filled with lines and he has pale, blue eyes. He had a hint of a blonde mustache and a little darker growth on his chin.

"Thanks." The kid, or maybe better described as a crazy bum, stretches, takes the lighter and lights his smoke. He stands up and spreads his arms.

"So, what's going on?" He asks as though he and Tommy had known each other for years.

"Nothin'. Just going to the beach."

"Y'know Arab?"

"Yeah, sure."

"Yeah, me and him go back years. You a train hopper?"

Tommy thinks to himself.

"Not that I'm trying to intrude." The kid's voice goes up an octave.

"Not really, it's fine."

"Just another kid?"

"Yeah, yeah," Tommy has some weird feelings. He doesn't normally associate with the other bums in the area, at least not the ones dressed like this. He is out in the world, but very protective of himself. Joe had always been there with him and he called most of these older street heads crazy. He didn't even approve of selling them drugs, but when he did he always made it clear to them that Tommy was off limits, like this was prison. Tommy had to admit that while he didn't see any danger, he was grateful for the protection.

There were a lot of kids, street kids, that just lounged around all day in parks, selling drugs and getting into drama. A lot of them lived at group homes, and such, but there was something feral to them that no system could tame and Joe seemed to have sensed this somehow and steered Tommy clear.

To be honest, Tommy didn't really see the harm of hanging out with them. He was often in the same park, doing the same thing, but he accepted Joe's judgment. Wasn't it funny to accept some advice and not others?

"Well, let me tell you something," the current street kid starts his monologue. "A man is running from a tiger, see, and suddenly falls off a cliff. He grabs onto a plant in the cliff's side and looks up. The tiger is still there and then he looks down... and there's another tiger!" At this point, the kid draws in a big hit off his tobacco and lets it out through his nostrils.

"He realizes he's about to die. Then he sees a small strawberry on the plant he's hung by, just barely ripe," the kid continues. "He grabs it and eats it and it's like the sweetest, best strawberry he's ever had..."

Tommy nods. He'd heard the story before. Back home somewhere.

"Yeah," he says.

"Pretty nice thing to say to someone you're about to kill."

Tommy looks up sharply, but the kid just smiles at him. Moments pass and finally the bus comes. Tommy gets on it and never looks back.

4.

When he gets off the bus to take a walk on the sunny boardwalk, Tommy doesn't really have any clue as to where he is going, for who, or what, or any plan or objective. His first object of interest was a pay phone for which he dug out some quarters to call Stephanie. No one picks up. He starts to formalize his plan: get something to eat, sun a little, maybe take a walk along the pier. Tommy hums for a minute as he feels the tight ball of black tar he'd taken from Stephanie's stash. He doesn't have any works, but he does have a small vial of water. Just a quick minute to dissolve the whole mess then snort it through his nose. It wasn't as awesome as the rush of injection, but he's trying to get off this shit.

Springtime is still hot as hell as far as he's concerned, but there aren't that many people on the beach. He just needs to kill a couple hours, then he'll call Stephanie and finalize their plans for the night.

He scans the beach for Arab, but only sees a couple maybes and it was clear as he walked towards them that they were not, in fact, the towering Jamaican and unlikely friend that Tommy had made so many months ago. Forgetting any thoughts of food, Tommy's footsteps bring him to the pier.

He sees Zeke leaning against a railing. He does not look well and as Tommy draws closer he could clearly see that Zeke was both high and drunk.

"Hi, Zeke," he mumbles as he draws alongside him at the railing. It wasn't that Tommy had lost his fear of the older drug-head, it was just that nothing had happened. Nothing had changed. The ocean waves stutter at the shore, held back by some kind of undertow. Tommy had learned a bit about the ocean since being there. Zeke looks over.

"Oh, Tommy, I didn't think I'd see you…" He trails off then wipes his face. His gaze returns to the sea.

"Everything ok?"

"Hmm? Oh, it's fine, fine…" The ocean waves keep coming. The sun is still bright, it's about four in the afternoon.

"I saw you leave," Zeke says. "But I was too fuckin' sick." He spit. "Heavy doses not helping a lot these days."

"I thought you were asleep."

"Oh, y'know, I don't sleep much, just rest, it's why I gotta have my medicine." Zeke suddenly gags and spits again. A pile of mucus makes its way into the ocean current.

"I'm good now," he says. "Just picked up my quota, maybe got a little too high. Why do we pick up here? It's just begging to be caught." Zeke's eyes turn to the water. "It is beautiful though," he sighs.

Tommy remains silent, shocked by this reflective Zeke. He had always seemed bigger than life, just a tough English cowboy coming up in an American paradise.

"I gotta tell you," Zeke says weakly. "We talk about you a lot."

"What? Me and Joe?"

"No, just you," Zeke smiles with thin lips barely divided by small white teeth. "Joe is, well, Joe has been around, but you. You don't make any moves. You just stay steady, comin' over and such, y'know, it's gotten to be a fairly popular topic, y'know?"

"Yeah," Tommy feels uncomfortably young. "Sisi mentioned something about it."

"Yeah? Yeah. Sisi is my world. I'd be nothing without her."

Tommy stays quiet. Eventually Zeke pushes himself from the railing.

"Do you wanna come over?"

"No, I got some stuff to do."

"Well, so long then. The next kilo will be coming in a day or two."

"Cool."

"Alright. I'll see you," he limps off and Tommy watches him stumble down the pier, presumably to his car. Wild.

*   *   *

About an hour later, Tommy watches for Stephanie's car. The evening is a little windy, but nothing like a storm or anything. There had been a few of those. Tommy had weathered them under small awnings from time to time and they were so unpredictable that one could never tell when a perfect day was going to be ruined. The rain could just pile down for an hour or two and they always seemed to come at night while Tommy was resting on his sleeping bag in an alley or on a roof. Whenever it happened, Tommy had to put it down to bad luck. He didn't take them seriously. Some people say that bad weather is proof that god hated them.

A few minutes later, Stephanie shows up and Tommy hops in her car. She kisses him as he pulls at his seatbelt.

"We're going out tonight."

"Should I shower? I've been up all day in the sun."

"No, it's fine. It's this new restaurant my friend told me about. We're going to chaperone her with this guy. It's about 15 minutes away. Don't worry."

"Oh," Tommy feels a little peaked, too much sun, but the thought of a meal quickly alleviates his nausea. He realizes the whole day has gone by and he hasn't eaten anything.

"I think you look fine," Stephanie continues as they sit in traffic. A drop of rain hits the windshield. Oh boy, thinks Tommy, here it comes. Sure enough, the one drop quickly turns into a thousand. There is no thunder, just pouring rain. Stephanie navigates through it while Tommy stares out the dripping passenger window.

Nothing is really working, he thinks. It seems he has magically gotten into a good relationship, stable and such, but it's only been a few days since Stephanie's heroin junkie, addiction blues incident.

Stephanie seems happy, but in that fake, bubbly, kind of way. Like any junkie that has been told she can continue her addiction. She certainly has been paying more attention to him, but it really just reminds him of Gina. Just a "keeping up appearances" kind of date. Not that he is getting out. He feels the ball of tar again.

He hardly thinks of Sisi and if he is being totally honest with himself, this is surely the best time he's had in months. That's got to be something, he thinks.

He tries to picture what it was he thought he was getting into when he moved west. Fast cars, he thinks. Skydiving, scuba diving, lots of drugs. Cars with sunroofs. Sitting by the sea. It was like he'd been deluded or something. He knew from visiting Boston and Providence that life was tough, but the kids he'd talked to seemed happy. He worried that by not reaching out he was missing something. Sunsets in an endless summer of freedom. He wonders if he'd ever even tried to think it through. He had been just so lonely.

It had only gotten worse through high school. He found himself staring out the passenger side of his mom's van to imagine himself in every eighteen-wheeler that they passed. He thought about how he would joke and tell stories that he had accumulated through his years as a traveler. Surfing on the Pacific, surrounded by a tough team of fellow travelers.

When he heard Nirvana for the first time he'd been hooked. Surely this was the exit he was looking for. Partying till dawn in basement clubs and towering penthouses. Laughing at life because he was living it to its fullest, free and young. But had he become young and dumb?

He doesn't know if his new scene is anywhere close, but he feels like he's coming to a cliff. If things go wrong, maybe he'd be jettisoned to something better. If Stephanie and him fall out, he thinks.

Outside, the rain had stopped and the evidence of its downfall was rapidly drying, but there was a sense of cleanliness that wasn't there before. What was going on in Tommy's head though, was far from tidy.

If Zeke dies of an overdose. If Joe shows up with enough marijuana to keep them rich for life. If the cops pick him up for panhandling and then drug possession. If some crazed psycho starts killing street kids. If he gets a job or goes to an agency to live in a group facility.

Everything is so blurry now, but he sees dead ends everywhere. If he just goes back home.

He glances at Stephanie who was concentrating on the road in front of her. What if they just rode off and never looked back? Gina never would have done it and he doubted Sisi would either, but Stephanie…

It was all he could do to stop from screaming when "All Apologies" suddenly comes on the radio. Stephanie turns it up.

"How are you with this?" she shouts.

"It's fun," says Tommy. "Really, I'm having fun."

"You just look a little, I don't know, is defocused the word?"

"No, it's fine, I'm just tired." And he is. With everything. Hadn't she just said he looked fine?

They get to the restaurant and Stephanie spots her friend before she parks.

"Hi-ee!" she screams thought the window while Tommy stares straight ahead. "Be there in a min!" They park the car and Stephanie rushes out to embrace her friend. "Is he here yet?"

"No, but he should be here soon. Can you believe he asked me right at the beginning of class? He's so cute though, I'm really excited." The two talk for a few more minutes as Tommy stands awkwardly. He thinks about having a smoke, but it didn't seem appropriate. However, he finds his right hand going to his pocket and as the greeting meeting ends, he is lighting up.

"And this, is Tommy," says Stephanie. Her friend smiles. "Oh, you're just so cool," she says sarcastically. Tommy shrugs.

"This, Tommy, is Marie and we're waiting for Alex…"

"Right," Tommy exhales a plume of smoke. "You go in, I'll finish this and meet you."

"Ok," says Stephanie, then turns to put an arm around Marie's shoulder and giggles as Marie murmurs something about school or something. Tommy doesn't care at all.

As he stands on the sidewalk, he notices a couple of others loitering nearby. Trying not to be intrusive, he blows the smoke away from them.

"Hey man!" says one of them, a white guy with a goatee. "You want any?"

He is holding a joint, and Tommy kind of smiles and shakes his head.

"Just five bucks, best stuff in the world, man, if you know what I mean…?" says the dealer. Just then another man in dress pants steps up to the restaurant.

"Hey, you Alex?" Tommy asks him, ignoring the request from the other two.

"Yeah, you are?"

"Tommy, Stephanie's boyfriend."

"Oh great, good to meet you!"

"Hey man, wanna pull off of this?"

"They're inside, I'll be in soon."

"Hey man, I'm talking to you!" The tone is suddenly aggressive and Tommy looks back in alarm, but Alex just looks over.

"Sorry man," he says. "Not tonight."

"I just wanted you to acknowledge me," the man mumbles.

"We do, just kind of busy right now."

"Well, what about this guy?" Tommy realizes they were talking about him.

"It's cool, we're cool, Ok?" Alex says, then looks over his shoulder towards the restaurant. "It's cool, right?"

"I guess so." The weed dealer turns back to his companion.

"Well," says Alex. "Should we go in?"

"Yeah," says Tommy, flicking the cigarette into the street. "Yeah, let's go." Feeling kind of awed by the whole scene, Tommy follows this confident figure.

The inside of the restaurant is made up of about ten booths off to each side of the room. There are two high tables in the center surrounded by stools and art on the wall. Along the door to the kitchen there is a beam painted blue and yellow and says something in a foreign language. Tommy and Alex spot their dates in the middle booth, on the left side.

"Hey-Oh!" shouts Alex when he spots them and approaches the table. Tommy comes up alongside him.

"Are you fine ladies eating alone?" jokes Alex and Marie

giggles as she looks down blushing. Stephanie smiles like a polite host.

"You must be Alex," she says, reaching out a hand as Tommy turns to enter the booth. "Charmed, I'm sure."

"How did you guess?"

"Oh, your height and weight and hair color. And, of course, your sense of style."

"Hmm," says Marie. "He dresses like that all the time.

"It's kind of my uniform," says Alex. "May I sit?" Tommy had already shoved his way onto the cushioned chair, banging his head on the tall barrier between the booths. He reflects that even the bravest man could be a douche. Who was this guy kidding?

Marie laughs as her handsome prince descends into the night with jokes, anecdotes, personal stories and not more than a dozen compliments. Tommy thinks about everything that had happened to him that day and how absolutely none of it was relevant, or polite to bring up. He stays silent. Stephanie drinks two glasses of white wine which she'd procured with a fake ID. The rest drink soda.

It was funny because everything that Alex said seemed to front him as an alpha-man, but he never brought up conflict, just deep thoughts about the news usually preceded by what he's seen at various screening of French Noir films, which made him sound more and more sophisticated. What could Tommy say? That dry air made him blow blood out of his nose? The man never said anything real, the least bit shady, or a word about drugs and Tommy felt out of his league.

When the check came, Alex picked it up without any thought to Marie and Stephanie's objections that the bill should be separate. Tommy feels the crisp twenties in his wallet but says nothing.

Outside, the two bystanders had vanished and after some chit-chat over cigarettes, everyone apparently had them, they just weren't as addicted as Tommy, the couples say their goodbyes. It takes all types, reflects Tommy and rides home in a fairly good mood. Stephanie goes to bed while Tommy takes a shower and when he gets to the bed, he finds her sleeping.

Unfortunately, thinks Tommy, not all types get laid. As she sleeps, he takes half the ball of tar and snorts. Life wasn't that bad after all.

5.

Course, it isn't as if Tommy is a bore. He has some sterling qualities, not the least of them is having a disarming smile. When he walks past stops in all of LA, he is sometimes greeted by well-wishers. He is what middle class folks call "good homeless." He is clean, doesn't harass customers; he has something of a hardened look that makes his age uncertain. During the day he is Tommy, just trying to live life. At night, he is a drug dealer and maybe a few weekends in between.

He is far from his punk dream. He admits this. Somehow it had been hijacked by Joe and his philosophies of survival, which he now knew were really just a protection of his investment in a drug dealing partner he could short to play a more lucrative drug running game. Tommy'd been used and spit out to a less ambitious druggie, Zeke.

The only difference between him and those two is that that Joe and Zeke go through their lives like it's a party and Tommy is just figuring it out. For some reason, he can't seem to let go and live. He guesses you have to be on top to do that.

Whatever, not important.

As it is, now he finds himself sleepless, laying on a bed, remembering the humiliation of his night out. A failure by all counts. He's not even high, just not sick. His stomach still hurts, but that's about the extent of it. He's existing at the exact amount of pain that he can handle.

Tommy had come to L.A. to live an American punk rock dream and all he'd ended up with were a bunch of experiences he couldn't talk about in modern day society, not even to Stephanie.

Every day the hounds are getting closer, he thinks. Every day he sees a cop car pass. Everyday a disgruntled face in a suit. He wants to scream because even if they aren't on to him, he feels their icy cold fingers around his neck and even heroin couldn't completely eclipse his paranoia.

He remembers sitting at one corner in an obscure part of the city close to the bus system. All of a sudden what had been an empty corner was teaming with black men. One grabbed him while another patted him down.

"You a cop? You a cop?"

He mumbled 'no' to this and they left as quickly as they had come, cigarettes at his feet, some of his own, some a different brand. The last thing he saw was one kid, maybe 12 years-old looking back at him and spitting on the ground.

But that was just it! How do you explain something like that? How do you state it? What if it wasn't just that corner, but every one? Tommy had kept it to himself and never went back to that spot. He was aware that there were gangs, several people had mentioned it to him, but during the day he'd felt bullet proof. Even now. He was untouchable. An American archetype. In torn jeans and T-shirts. He was getting more and more popular as the year went by. Nirvana had taken care of that.

And, anyway, what was going on with that band? Were they breaking up, reconciling, just tired and heavy on remaining true, or had they, too, sold out to the mega-corporations and illiterate rednecks that Tommy and all his friends had sarcastically called jocks. Yeah, they bought the records, but they had no idea who, for instance, Leonard Cohen was.

What's with the dollar on a fish-hook? If you have to ask, you'll never know, thinks Tommy, but even to him it's becoming more and more blurry where the action is.

As for options, there aren't a lot. He'd noticed more curious stares from young women and almost jealousy and disgust from young men. But what to do about that? Could he bust through all that resentment and just go? No, plans, just hitch out of this town? He had totally struck out tonight, but all in all… Stephanie believed in him, he thinks, then puts himself down.

It's completely insane, he thinks as he turns to sleep. Totally delusional. It had taken a lot just to get here, now how long would it take to get out?

He didn't have a game, or a rap, he breathes sleepily, happy to know the heroin was doing its job, happy to know he was alive. He's just living a real life and by and large, he loves it, he thinks to himself. Sure, any of that other stuff would be easy enough to get into. Of course, there are the dreams…

*   *   *

Sisi and Tommy make out in the back of a mini-van. Kurt watches in a bored silence, smoking a cigarette. In the front, Joe and his girlfriend are arguing.

"We took the wrong exit, this doesn't go anywhere," Joe says sarcastically.

"You're the one with the map," she replies with equal amount of aggression.

"Well, turn around."

"I think there's a road up here."

"You know what's gonna happen," says Kurt. Tommy pulls himself out of Sisi's mouth.

"You know we're going to crash."

"I don't know! You're not even real!"

"I know, but so do you."

"Ok, fine, I'll turn in this driveway," Joe's girlfriend says in a high snarl.

"You don't have to be so mean about it."

The car tilts as she pulls into the driveway, backs up sharply and then takes off.

"You know what's going to happen."

Just then there was a sharp bump and Tommy shoves his face into Sisi's neck.

"I don't know, I don't know, I don't!"

"You know," says Kurt, taking another drag off his smoke. "You have always known."

*   *   *

"So, what do you think?" asks Kurt. He is sitting on some grass. Sisi is gone. Cars have pulled over and paramedics are pushing the mother into an ambulance.

"I think you know pretty damn well what I'm thinking!"

Tommy growls back.

"You can't go on this way. People are beginning to notice." A flock of birds break out of the trees as Joe's girlfriend is put in handcuffs. "You're gonna be picked up."

"Like one of your CDs right? Pretty strong talk for someone who's just got to worry about the next magazine he's talking to!"

"You're gonna be in a magazine article on homeless youth." Tommy exhales quickly.

"So, what? I'm doing ok now, I've got a life." Stephanie runs by in a sundress chasing a Frisbee. Slowly, the scene of loss and despair dissipates and the two are talking in an open field.

"It's not just that, it's your mind. Have you noticed how real I've become? I'm practically in charge of every scene you're in, just you aren't there! You are so lazy you're letting your mind take over you!"

"And what would you have me do about it?"

"I don't know. Go to a concert, listen to some music, get out of this place. I may be here, but I'm not a lot too. I can get away with anything because I'm just in your head. You gotta understand, this isn't for kids!"

"Yeah, yeah." Tommy watches Julia doing cartwheels, heavy make-up and tight jeans with frayed marks on the knees and a flannel patterned T shirt. Jewelry hangs from her neck and ears.

"If you'd just get out more…"

"Like I haven't tried. The double date was a disaster, I've tried the beach, the desert, the streets, the apartments, hell, I thought I was ready to go back to school for a minute…"

"Maybe you should just be a regular kid. Go home or go to Skid Row. That's where all the other homeless kids go. Talk to someone who isn't your girlfriend. You're too isolated. This is your chance to tour the world, eat up!"

Tommy shakes his head. The sky is wildly turning purple, green and there are all these girls all around doing somersaults and cartwheels.

"I don't know."

"Just do me a favor and lighten up."

"Ok, I'll try."

*   *   *

True to his word, Zeke's kilo comes in and he's willing to share. Sisi isn't there in the late morning and Zeke just breaks up the drugs into separate baggies.

"You'll owe me another bill starting tomorrow," says Zeke, gruffly. Tommy had already paid for the last front. To be honest, Tommy wonders if his mere presence is payment enough. He noticed that the price had gone down. He's pretty sure that's because Joe had lied and saved up enough money to put a stake down for another van-full of weed, but, shit, if the whole thing didn't make Tommy feel like he's looking after a charity case.

Zeke looks absolutely awful. His hair is growing in patches along his jaw-line. His eyes are bloodshot. His breath stinks. If there was ever a moment for a crown prince to murder his father and take the throne, it is now.

"I'm going out," Zeke continues, but stops suddenly to scratch his neck. "You good on holding on to this till night?" Tommy nods. He had vague plans to visit a park and maybe get some more whiskey. A stack of fives and ones are in his wallet and he just wants to relax. Perhaps he's getting soft.

Zeke continues to separate the property, sometimes licking his fingers. It was almost frightening how low Zeke had come. Just trying to beat his illness before an afternoon shot, Tommy figures.

"Ok, I'll see you later." Tommy sticks the evidence in the bottom of his pack. While Zeke looks for his keys, Tommy sneaks back out onto the street. He stands still and listens to the birds, then to Zeke's car coming to life and driving off in the other direction. He hums a little tune while smoking his cigarette then heads for his now familiar bus stop. He almost decides to double back to wait for Sisi, but there was always that chance that Zeke would return high and inquisitive. He wonders where Mike is.

As the sun rises in the sky, Tommy boards his bus and decides to go straight to Hollywood and maybe get some lunch. He is in fine control of his situation. A young bum who rooms at his girlfriend's house sometimes and sleeps anywhere else he wants on others. Today, he wears a clean shirt and pants with raggedy sneakers. If he wastes his time enough, he can get over the day's hump and hustle for the night.

Things went well in that way. The bus breaks down and the driver has to call in another. Tommy spends the next hour listening to people grumble, some in Spanish and others in a California dialect. He takes a seat on the sidewalk and chain smokes until the new bus arrives.

If he went along the side streets of Hollywood, he'd probably still be bored and alone when four o'clock hit, so he scraps that idea and when the bus parks, he heads in the opposite direction of the restaurants and bars towards the desert mountain with its big sign proclaiming a name that speaks volumes of the arrogance of its builders.

Hollywood.

Just about the hottest place on earth to come up. He walks past street performers and residents tredding along with probably just the same outlook as he has. Bored. Disillusioned.

He starts to climb up the winding road, but quickly gets tired and sits down to munch on some granola bars and drink bottled water. He'd snorted some dope earlier, Stephanie had gone out and bought another bag of it. They both agreed that if they didn't shoot up, they couldn't get sick. It was an anthem as close to their heart as "always be prepared."

Just then, a small-scooter whizzes by with two figures on it, an aging man and a twenty something boy with long hair and a screwed up face, bracing in the wind. The two quickly get out of sight. Tommy sighs and gets up again.

About an hour later he sits against a viewing area with his back to the sign. A few people mill around, mostly tourists, snapping pictures, but also a few couples hold hands and walk around the platform without really looking up, or around.

Tommy spots a thirty-something pair in all black, just smoking cigarettes and leaning on the rail with their backs to the sign as well, but he doesn't approach them. It's really hot to be wearing black, he thinks. He forces himself to light another cigarette and drink water.

The couple don't appear to be having much fun. Occasionally, the girl would say something too far away to hear and then flick her cigarette. The man didn't appear to say anything at all. Not even a grunt. Tommy watches them and thinks that they are bohemians and then quickly decides that they must be actors, or writers, or something creative. The woman has earrings shaped like ankhs. But they're here, thinks Tommy. Into something he can't figure out.

Someday, maybe, one or both of them would be famous and he'd see them in magazines. They'd be musicians, or set designers, or poets. Whatever it is, he feels it exuding off of them like hot, red flames. And it's not just the sun talking, he thinks.

The couple eventually leaves and it is about four, so Tommy gets up, takes a look at the sign then tumbles his way down the road, occasionally stopping to survey his surroundings and smoke another cigarette as well as drink a third bottle of water. About an hour later he was back to sea level and walks to a sushi joint where he eats some, drinks water, uses the bathroom and then moves towards the top of the restaurant to watch people from a balcony.

He sips lemonade and finally his alias, a rich actor of some sort, fades and he becomes, once again a homeless drug dealer. He walks to the club and slides into the alley. It is just all scenery, he thinks and throws his pack behind the dumpster then walks to the entrance of the alley and stretches in the setting sun.

PART V

Evening comes on. Tommy sits on the opposite side of the dumpster between a fence and a pile of bottles. He doesn't really care if his jeans get a little sticky. He squats by the walls of the club. Smoking a cigarette. The night should be a good one. If he makes enough money, he'll be good for another week of high-living. Maybe this time he'd smarten up and get a job somewhere. It was just… At this point he realizes he's making a lot more money dealing drugs than say being a clerk at 7-11. It's just unpredictable. He prays, as he always does that he doesn't get arrested that night.

Then he hears a noise. At first, he thinks maybe it's an employee throwing away the trash, or a rat, but then a voice springs out of the emptiness.

"Hey, hey! Are you here?"

"What?" Tommy gets up and walks to the front of the alley. It's the big man and behind him, a couple of bartenders. Athletic and muscular looking.

"Good. You're here."

"Yeah?"

"Listen, I'm gonna have to ask you to leave." Tommy stares at him.

"Like last week you were here… I thought I saw something in

you, but I can't have you selling here. They're getting on us about underage drinking, for Christ's sake…"

"Well," Tommy says. "It's up to you."

"Listen, I'll buy everything you have. 200 bucks sound good?"

Tommy nods. Everything was coming apart in his head, but he remains calm, He pulls out the drugs out of his pack, all carefully spaced sacks of plastic in a larger shopping bag.

"Sure," he says.

"That's what I'm talking about! Y'know, kid, I have a proposition for you. Come back tomorrow and buy a suit. We need people like you." Tommy watches as the big guy puts the bag beneath his arm to take his wallet out of his pants.

"There you go," he says, "200 for the stuff and an extra 100 for the suit. Show up at this time… I got some work for you."

Tommy doesn't know what to say.

"Thanks," he finally says, picks up his pack and walks past the three men in a sullen slouch. The big man watches him go and one of the bartenders takes out a cigarette. What the fuck is this all about?

*   *   *

That night Tommy talks Stephanie into going to the beach. They bring a blanket and a case of beer and just bundle up under the bright sky of the city. It's an anniversary of sorts, but neither of them take much truck in that kind of thing. They're happy just in the moment. They'd abstained from their stash of dope for an entire day.

Tommy cracks open a beer while Stephanie puts on a sweater.

The two of them just gaze at the water and watch distant points
of light in the sky. It's well after midnight. The two of them had
spent a couple hours making love in the apartment. Now they
were just chilling out. No words expressed themselves.

Tommy wants to talk about his new "work" but he keeps
silent. Where in god's name was he going to store the suits? He's a
little confused about the entire endeavor. If the big guy was catching flak about underage drinkers, how could hiring one be at all
wise? Things just happen, he figures. Far from being just another
reoccurring thought, it was this statement that was scaring him
now. But the money...

Stephanie seems happy. She looks up at the sky without
smiling, but her eyes are fixed on the horizon with her arms
propping up her body behind her. The breeze along the coast is a
little strong, but she doesn't seem affected by it. They listen to the
sound of the ocean. Watch the lights on the pier grow dim. Just
like when they first met, actually. Tommy feels the first stirrings
of joy.

They sit there for another hour. Then they walk hand in hand
back to the car.

*   *   *

So, Tommy shows up the following night wearing jeans and a
T-shirt, holding a suit. For some reason, he'd decided not to wear
the suit on the bus, but was then perplexed as to how to get it into
the club at all. In a flurry of indecision and pacing back at Stephanie's house, late, he finally gets his mind around leaving his pack,
puts on his cleanest clothes and transports the suit, hanger and

all, by hand. Yes, he'd gotten a lot of weird looks, but not as many as if he'd worn it.

It was a really nice suit.

He didn't think Stephanie had noticed it in the linen closet, had no idea where to hide it next. It was weird, but everything was weird about this double-life he was leading. Maybe it was just something he had to get used to, he thinks. If this "job" works out.

The club isn't open when he gets there, but he pounds on the door four or five times and one of the bartenders opens it. She is a pretty girl with pink curls and a black dress on. She looks at him with dead eyes, then turns to listen to a voice Tommy can't hear because it's so indistinct.

"Come in," she says and Tommy takes his first steps into the building as an employee.

"He's in the back," says the girl from behind him. Tommy nods and walks towards the stage. Behind the curtain he could hear some sounds, so he carefully pulls it upward and crawls by one light into a hallway which holds a couple of doors. Uncertain, he listens first, then picks a door when he's sure that there is indeed someone behind it. He knocks and hears the sound of someone saying goodbye and hanging up the phone. The door opens. It's the big man.

"Good to see you," he mumbles and turns back towards a vanity on the far side of a very small room. "Come in," he says.

Tommy takes some unsure steps into the room, then seeing that no one else was there, brings the suit down off his shoulder and stands awkwardly.

"Close the door," says the big man, taking note of the suit still in a plastic shroud. "I'm glad you could make it." He holds up a mirror.

"Want some?" Tommy shakes his head.

"Good, not a party guy, just work for you, eh?" Tommy doesn't know what to say, so he just nods.

"Well, here it is. You're comin' inside. I want you to get dressed and stand in the hall. It's the same thing, but you'll be hidden in a room and I'm the only one you have to say 'boo' to. The only reason you'll see anyone else is if I'm bringing you some work. Do you know what I mean?" Tommy stares, perplexed.

"By work, I mean I'm bringing you some bodies, understand? I'll be bringing in some young punk that I want you to take out." Tommy stares at him, his facing going pale. The big man just sits there, then a slow grin picks its way on his face.

"Hah, I had you going... no seriously, there's a door in the back that leads to the outside, opposite side of the building. When I knock like this," he hits the vanity three times with his knuckles. "Then I want you to go outside. I'll bring the son of a bitch around the club and you hide behind the door, come out and just beat the shit out of them with this," he holds up a bat.

"Here's a mask too, I just want you to give them a reason to not return, ok?" Tommy swallows hard, then nods in a shuddering kind of way.

"Ok, I'll get out of your way. Worst comes to worst, I'll put you in the bathroom and say you're a guard or something. Just don't get blood on that. Ok? Ok... see you in a minute." The big man snorts another line then gets up and pats Tommy on the back.

"Don't worry, you won't have to do this often." He smiles and brushes past to the door. Tommy stares after him and then shortly gets into his new uniform. This is alright, he tells himself, and quickly walks out of the dressing room.

2.

The night arrives. Tommy waits in what amounts to a closet with a door leading in and a door going out. He sits, bored now after the initial shock and spends a good amount of time examining his bat. It's wooden and fairly new. He can't imagine hitting someone in the head with it, but he practices shoving it like a spear into someone's chest, then bringing it around to break a kneecap. He still has no idea what he's gotten himself into. Is it some kind of joke? Why the hell does he need a suit to do this? The big man had left the bag of drugs with him, but it was a bit lighter.

Basically, Tommy has to figure, the man had just gone insane, was in danger of losing his license and was blaming it all on the young kids getting served. It made a certain kind of sense, he thinks, plus the low price of only twice marked-up of drugs that even Tommy had to admit were pretty damn good, came into the equation. Some people can't control themselves, he decides. Even those like himself.

He doesn't have to do anything this time though. The big man unlocks the door from the outside only eight times, hurrying in, grabbing the baggie from Tommy's hand, thanking him, then turning out the door which Tommy locks behind him. Very simple.

At the end of the shift, the big man gives him 200 dollars then tells him to leave the suit in the dressing room and it'd be cleaned for the next weekend. After saying goodbye, Tommy marches to a payphone and calls up Stephanie feeling like a winner.

*   *   *

"Does that feel good?"

Stephanie leans over Tommy's back, rubbing his shoulders, his back and his thighs, Tommy has his eyes closed. They'd been laying there all day, snorting and licking powder off each other's naked bodies.

"Mmm, feels good," he sighs. Things were going well. Stephanie took the day off, something about not needing a review and by the way she was treating him, he fully agreed. School was a waste, he thinks, then sighs again. It was all coming back to him.

His sudden lift in income has let him reconnect with his original views. If a kid like him could make 400 in a week? Shit, all this ideology, to be 'the leaders of society' it made no sense because it was where he was that really mattered. It was the real world and it wasn't going to change no matter how many anthologies you read, theories you studied. Just look at Stephanie, supposedly a student headed for bigger and better sniffing heroin off her boyfriend's back? The new world was here and now and it was going to take people like Tommy to lead it.

Look at all the dissatisfaction that plagued the world, he thinks. The wars, the diseases, the general feeling that rocked even a poor refugee a million miles away into taking up a gun and shooting other kids while deluded christians talked on TV about needing only pennies a day! Tommy had talked about it all night, just swigging beers and smoking cigarettes in their bedroom. Stephanie really got it too. She smoked a joint and smiled over his naked body. They were going to make it.

"Sure, you don't want a hit of this?"

"No, no. I'm good." And it was true. He didn't need pot to fuck up his new-found vision. If scientists were correct, then there were plenty of hormones rushing in him already, and the dope made him last for hours. Speaking of that.

"Do you wanna make it?" He props up on his elbows and stretches.

"Whatever you want," she says, huskily enunciating each syllable. Tommy laughs nervously. Somehow, he was always afraid of a horny girl. It was weird because what else did a red blooded American boy want? He flips over and lets her do her work all over his body.

*   *   *

The next day she dresses and walks around the bedroom while he lays tangled in sheets watching her female form rush to and fro. This is a scene he could live over infinite amounts of time, he thinks. He takes another pull off his tailor-made smoke and lets it fill the room with second-hand cancer.

"I'm really sorry, honey," she says as she pulls on stockings, "But I'm an independent woman, right? I gotta feed the man so he feeds me." Tommy doesn't answer, but he feels quite the pimp. Sure, I mean, she isn't going out to walk the streets, but he doesn't control her. It's all a part of his enlightened world view. He isn't a bully and she isn't his. She just picked him and it feels so good.

"Don't be long," he smiles.

"I'll see you when I see you. I can't cage you up. Call around six, ok?"

"Sounds good."

"Alright, bye honey."

"Bye, sweetheart." And she leaves again. Women, thinks Tommy, then gets out of bed, dragging the sheet to the hamper, then sauntering naked into the hall and then the bathroom. As hot water pours over his body, he closes his eyes. Then the whisper began.

"What are you doing?" asks the voice.

"Just waiting," Tommy keeps his reply silent, just willing the words in his mind.

"Are you serious?" the voice reminds Tommy of Kurt Cobain. He pauses a moment, then says aloud.

"I don't think I need you anymore."

"Don't need me? I don't need you, but this isn't what I wrote all those songs for. It was supposed to satisfy you till you're old enough to be on your own, not inspire you to be, well you."

"I said, I don't need you!"

"Alright, fine." The water keeps falling, but Tommy is now crunched up in a fetal position on the floor. He stays that way until the water becomes cold, then shuts off the valve and walks back into the hallway to a closet that houses linens. He buries his face in a white towel. He goes back into the bedroom and doesn't emerge for a long while.

*   *   *

He must've walked an hour from Stephanie's collegiate en-
closure before he could get the nerve up to stop and access the
situation. He was crazy, obviously. Very damaged from something
and all the oddities that had piled up since childhood leading to
his odyssey across the States… Now, too many drugs, hard living,
adjusting his personality to the constraints of independence…
not fun, pretty scary, actually.

He knows that the world hasn't changed, just himself, a million neurons shooting right up to a dope center in his brain. The
next bus he catches is one straight to Zeke's neighborhood. Just
one connecting route.

He walks the blocks leading to Zeke's domain, painfully
realizing that his feet really aren't used to this much activity and
he doesn't have any socks on, just boots, shorts and a long sleeve
flannel. For some reason, he feels a chill. The sun is setting and
Zeke's car isn't in the driveway. Good, he thinks, he just wants
to unwind without any drama. Just whiskey with water and the
soothing tones of an understanding ear. He is in love now, he
knows. Sisi is all he can focus on. He needs a strong woman for
his fractured mind.

He needs love and affection. A house he can live in to foster
his ego and get off of drugs, get a job, maybe go back to school.
And she needs him, too.

Stephanie wasn't working. He needed someone stronger,
more real. Stephanie could never understand. She idolized his
life, but he can't go on even for another night. All that talk was

bullshit. Even he, himself, can't comprehend all the garbage that had spilt out of his mind. Kurt was right, well, the Kurt he'd made up was right. This wasn't the way things should be. He makes his way to the house, just praying he'll be fixed.

But the lights in the house are out and slowly, Tommy turns around and makes his way back. The moon is full now, there's even some cajoling women on the Sunset Strip when he gets there, slowly rotating their hips in his direction, but he finds a bridge with a mattress under it to sleep it off. Things will be better, he tells himself, better for him, better for his mind, better for Stephanie... why had he ever thought less of her? Oh, it was time to black out now. Just simple exhaustion.

In the morning, he'd pick up his bones and get back to Stephanie's for his pack and make a real effort of making it. Put in an application at each storefront, buy another cheap suit and stroll the city like a real winner. Maybe then Kurt would go away. As soon as he's stable, he thinks and lets his mind go to oblivion.

*　　*　　*

Tommy wakes up in a few hours. No cars are on the road and no one else had come to sleep, so he walks back to the Strip and strolls the surrounding streets. The city is so quiet at what he judges to be three in the morning. He'd left his watch in his pack and he had no sense of time at night. He worries and wanders the alleys. Sees a few people sleeping in parking lots. He is truly alone in a city of dreams. He breathes deeply. The air is truly beautiful in the city's slumber and he walks under street lamps. Gradually he lets his mind calm and the terrors of the day world slip away, taking away residues of exhaustion and pure madness.

He turns a corner and spots a cop car idling in the road. He stops, then puts his hands in his pockets, searching for a cigarette. The car drives away without a glance and he wonders if he's invisible. The moon is also high in the sky and the signs they have up are blinking still. All these performers and bums and prostitutes are bereft of their domain and now it is his and his alone.

His attitude is neutral and blank. Sisi or Stephanie? Who cares, who really knows? It all comes back to him. The sweet night in any woman's arms whether it be Stephanie or Gina, or Sisi… And somewhere his mother sits at home, breathing heavily as everyone sleeps and stares at a wall. Tommy thinks he should call her and as if by magic he spots a payphone. It'd be tracked though, he thinks. So, he doesn't call home, he just sends a silent prayer.

He wasn't shirking though. He really intended to get clean, get out of the business, carve his own road. The past is irrelevant, but without Joe around, he probably never would've gotten to this cross-roads. Using drugs and bumming change, talking about going to raves and exotic locations but going nowhere, he'd missed that hurdle before. Now he could make the right choices and do the right thing…

But it hurt too much. Tommy tries to give himself a pep talk. Everything had gone insane, but he could mount an expedition to stability. He could stand on that rise as long as he anyone. He would dare to be different by being the same. Once he made it, he'd call his mom.

He shrugs his shoulder against the cold, puffs on his cigarette
and returns to the bridge. He gets there, sits on the mattress and
chain-smokes for the hours before sunrise. Then he walks to a
diner a-little-ways away, greets the cook and gets a coffee. The day
is ready to begin. He asks for an application to wash dishes.

The breakfast is good. Ham and eggs and toast, all with black
coffee. He gives the application back to the waitress and asks to
speak to the manager. She silently takes it back. A few minutes
later an elderly black woman walks out of the kitchen and she
catches Tommy's eye.

"I'm the manager. What can I do for you?"

Tommy looks at her blankly. He hadn't any plan and this was
new. He turns to look around her.

"I want to work," he says a moment later. "I think I could
be a real asset to your organization." The lady looks at him and
considers.

"Ever done this before?"

"Yeah, mostly at home though."

"Are you good?"

"I can clean a Thanksgiving day's load of pots and pans in less
than a half an hour."

"Well, that's a start."

"I'm really willing to make the effort to work out well here."

"I can see that. Listen, why don't you come in tomorrow. 8
o'clock ok?"

"I can start today…"

"I don't need that. I need reliable help. If you can do that, if you have what it takes to be here at all times, when I need you, then we'll see about hooking you up."

"I don't know what to say." She stares at him.

"Thank you, I'll be here," he says finally.

"Good, see you tomorrow."

3.

Just like that he gets up and walks out. He is onto something new and he doesn't want to ever give it up. He doesn't even question where his motivation comes from. He is alive and he is changing.

But the day wore on. He decides to go east and experience some desert. Not too far from Zeke's house, he gets off the bus and wanders around.

All the houses are low and residential. There are small plots of just overgrown desert plants and of course, the sun high in the sky. He doesn't spend much time, just 15 minutes to admire the strange world he finds himself in and smoke a couple of cigarettes. There is nothing like this back home and he feels almost content in the arid air. Stretching, he makes his way back to the bus and rides a long while to Stephanie's apartment. Like any junkie, he still needs his fix.

He gets off the bus and lugs himself home. Funny to think of it like that. Stephanie pulls up just as he gets to the door. No idea what he would've done without her. She smiles broadly as she gets out of the car with a flop straw hat on.

"Hope you're ready for some excitement," she says as she leans in close to kiss him on the cheek. "My roommate is on vacation starting today," she whispers in his ear. Dutifully, Tommy follows her to the bedroom and the scene fades out with "Serve the Servants" in the tape player of the stereo inside. What did he do to deserve all this?

*   *   *

So, the morning comes up and Tommy drags himself out of bed without waking Stephanie, puts on a pair of pants he'd bought and a plain white T-shirt. He pulls his hair up into a bun, snorts a line of dope and hits the road. By 7:30 he's in Hollywood again and pushes his way into the restaurant.

There are already some patrons in the place and Tommy stands awkwardly in the front door.

"You," says the cook. "Get back there." Still feeling out of place, Tommy walks into the back. It's a small kitchen with a lot of cooking spatulas and tongs on one wall and a big metal sink and a steel grill on the other. In the corner was a vent for fry grease. On the far wall is a mop in a bucket. Pimpled ceilings, tiled floors, white-stained walls and a door next to the sink.

"In there," says the cook, pointing with his thumb. Tommy takes a deep breath and opens the door.

The office is small, stacks of paper on the desk with a small timepiece on it and a couple of pictures. There's an old newspaper article in a frame on the wall. In back of the desk is his new employer.

"This," she says, pushing a folder across the table. Tommy looks at it. It's a small set of papers. Work papers. Papers that went through the tax people.

"Um," he says.

"Is not necessary," she finishes. She picks up the folder.

"This," she continues, building steam as she plows through the words, "is just another way to keep someone from starting anew. What are you, fifth-teen...?" she shakes her head. "I don't know who you are, or where you're from, or what you've been running from, but I can see desperation when it slaps me in the face."

"Eight dollars an hour, twenty hours a week, day or night. That's what I'm offering you."

"I..."

"And you'll take it. You have a place to stay? They haven't been collecting rent so this will be an improvement. Plus, your meals are free. This is the best deal you'll get. What's your name?"

"Uh, Tommy..."

"Tommy, good. This...," she gets up. "Is your job." She brushes past him. Tommy is stunned. Could he be talking to his savior?

"You will clean till your bones ache." In the kitchen now. The cook looks down at the meals on the grill, quickly puts one after another onto plates then carries five of them in two hands and bustles his way out of the kitchen. Ignoring him, his boss speaks on.

"He is your commander. Whenever he gets a pot greasy or a spoon hits the floor, it doesn't happen often, but still, you will pick it up, say 'thank you', clean it and deliver it back to him in tip top condition. Do I make myself clear?'

"Uh, yes, ma'am."

"My name is Suzy. You'll clock out at one."

"Uh, thank you."

"Thank you is quite enough. And when we see you on the silver screen, that'll be my moment."

"Er, yeah?"

"Definitely. Now, get to work. His name is cook and I'm Suzy… don't forget it."

"I won't." Taking one more look around the kitchen, she turns and leaves. Jesus, thinks Tommy. Now he has to work?

*   *   *

He scrubs and soaks and sprays. Really, it's not very hard, a fact which offsets the poor return and Tommy doesn't mind when the cook points to the fans above the grill. He takes them down as per the cook's gruff explanation and starts scouring the grease off them with a metal scrub-ball. The hours fly by. At the end of it, Suzy gives him two twenties and a plate of potatoes and eggs.

"Be back here tomorrow," she warns as he piles the food, plate to mouth without any real space in between.

"Ok," he says between bites.

If the Strip holds anything at one in the afternoon, it's sunlight and street people. Down the street is a youth shelter and that's where most of the "kids" go for breakfast, but some of them stay around the area. They were all casually dressed like him and Tommy spots a few "actors" getting into character for the day. If they just hang out enough, they'll be discovered, he thinks.

His work is done and Tommy heads downtown to his real job, begging on the street. Things have come into focus for him this morning. He'd continue his ridiculous farce of a life, but slowly edge his way to respectability. Some money to get a place with a room and work things out with Stephanie.

When he rises to a level of competence, when the two of them are clean, he'll call home and update the follies of his doings to his parents. It'll be a relief, he silently tells himself. No more running from the law. He'd get a job cleaning tables at another restaurant, he'd make it. Opportunity was bound to come his way.

While he wasn't an actor himself, Tommy wishes he could break into show business. That had been what motivated him to actually go to school. Maybe be a set maker, a boom-mic holder. It couldn't be that hard. Stephanie had taken some classes in the field, just trying to figure out what she wanted to do. He could take a class after he starts using his real name.

Then again, opportunity can knock at any time. He walks into a bar restaurant while the place is still opening. There's a balcony upstairs and servers putting together cloth napkins. He sidles up to the bar and asks for an application and a water. Both are brought tout de suite.

He's filling out an application when a trio of young artists bust in. They wave, animatedly to the bartender and take a seat at a table, taking out notebooks and head shots. Tommy listens to their conversations.

"So, if they say it's a go, I'll be set for…"

"No one knows about it, but it's the next big…"

"This new album will put them on top. I heard about this film interest…"

They're served sandwiches and shots. Breakfast of champions.

Tommy gets another water and passes in the application. One of the actors/artists/musicians stands next to him with a credit card.

"I got it today, Greg," he says sweetly, combing back his fashionable hair. The bartender says nothing but takes the card. The young man glances at Tommy.

"Whoa, hey man? Don't I know you?"

Tommy looks at him with unfocused eyes. He could be one in a million.

"Yeah, you, you hang out next to the club! What's up, brother!"

"Err, nothing, just trying to get a job," Tommy feels very tired all of a sudden.

"Dude, you'll be great. Give me a call if you need some spending money. I'll let you in, we'll party, shit, you can do some work. Look at those arms on you!" Tommy looks down to his biceps and flexes them briefly. He doesn't mind the attention, regardless of who it's from.

"Anyway, I'm not going to mess up your shit. Call me." The dude hands Tommy a card. It's cheap, just black on white, but it's something. Tommy smiles as he takes it.

"Thanks," he says, then looks towards the door. "I gotta go."

"Cheers! See you soon!"

Tommy walks out of the bar with a feeling of satisfaction and finds his way to the subway. It's going to be a good day.

*　　　*　　　*

Downtown holds some surprises as well. A couple denim wearing street punks are sitting on one corner opposite the subway and they give Tommy a friendly wave as he walks up.

"Hey," he says uncertain of what was going on.

"Oh, I'm sorry, we thought you were somebody else," one says. "Really, sorry."

"That's alright, what do you have going on?"

"Oh, nothing, just traveling through," says the other. Tommy mentally names them Gus and Matt. Doesn't know why.

"We've got some good home grown," says Gus, in a whispering tone.

"I'm good on that," says Tommy, looking over his shoulder. A couple of suits walk out of the subway, briefcases and everything, but most of the crowds are walking in the opposite direction.

"Yeah, kid?" says Matt. "You sure?"

"I'm good," says Tommy again, getting the inexplicable urge to move away, but finds himself trapped by social convention. "I'm not a cop," he says slowly. "But I don't do that."

"Gotta do something," mumbles Matt, but Gus smiles upwardly.

"I gotta go," says Tommy. "But thanks."

"May we meet again," smiles Gus. Tommy frowns a little then steps slowly away. The two are there all day. Tommy puts himself a block away and looks back at them every so often. There is something strange here.

4.

The days drag on, but Tommy feels good. He arrives at work at eight, every-day, scrubs through the morning, then breaks down on the pavement for an additional twenty-five to thirty dollars, enough to buy more clothes and laundry detergent. He's welcomed by Stephanie each night and the weekend whelms closer. They're doing less and less of the bag everyday.

After tasting the fruits of manual labor in a confined space, Tommy is well prepared for an all assaulting night at the club. He can't wait to club some useless drag on the party, just hit him a couple times. It's the newborn feelings of a productive member of society.

Of course, he has to secure the drugs for the evening, but he makes plans with Zeke after his shift.

Here's how that goes.

Tommy struts up to the house. He is fresh for his day job but had brought his pack to work at the grumblings of cook. It doesn't matter. Suzy had him put it in her office and everything was ok.

"You going to the laundromat?" she asks.

"Something like that," responds Tommy gracefully, he is really feeling good. Like a rocket ship to Mars.

"Well," says Suzy. "That's fine."

Now at Zeke's, Tommy immediately realizes that the dealer is not at home. His car isn't out front and there's evidence of a scuffle in the front yard. Tommy wonders how all this occurred, but quickly jogs up to the front door. He doesn't know how he feels about Sisi, his life has gone well without her and he has some real plans, but he realizes his waking point had been thanks to this brazen woman behind these doors, as well as the man in his head.

Sisi is in the kitchen as Tommy, smoothly and carefully, makes his way into the home.

"Hello?" she calls. "Zeke?"

"No, it's Tommy."

"Oh, hi Tommy! Zeke isn't here right now."

"Oh, um that's Ok. I just needed to discuss something with him. I can wait."

"Actually, he's going to be gone all day." Tommy's heart rate goes up a bit.

"Why don't I just tell him you came around? The usual things, right?"

"Uh, yeah." A bit of disappointment.

"Ok, he'll have it in two days."

"Uh, ok."

"I'll see you."

"Yeah, see you."

Tommy leaves with a lump in his throat. He hadn't realized how dependent he'd become of her approval. He'd sort of thought he could come in with triumphant energy and make out and who knows what else, but this brush off burns him to the core. Whatever. He'd get the stuff the usual way in two days.

He finds himself back at Stephanie's. He's taken the day off from begging. He and Stephanie hadn't talked about his sudden legitimacy and he doubted they would. She'd love him no matter what, he thinks bitterly. Not like a goddess, he thinks sullenly now. Not like a mother, just the result of the trusting bond between them now. It was all so shoddy, he thinks to himself. But she never asked where he went to everyday. Why was he being such an asshole?

He had a few dreams that night, mostly revolving around his family, his mother and father and sister. Pretty soon he'd be able to connect with them. He knew in his heart that things were going well. They'd be all fixed soon.

And there'd been no encounters with Kurt. The rock star had mysteriously disappeared and Tommy was grateful. It seemed like he'd gotten on the right track. The people at the diner had been friendly and Tommy looks forward to work each day. He also has that number from his newfound connection on the Strip and he comfortably held it in his mind that he was going places.

On the one particular morning, he wakes before Stephanie and stretches, considering all the things he had to do that day. He'd work, pick up from Zeke, maybe beg a little… He showers and brushes his teeth then comes back to the bedroom and just watches her. She is so beautiful, he thinks, then he picks up his pack and leaves to catch the bus. He is just so lucky! He actually considers not sneaking a line in the morning, that's how good he's feeling, but he brushes off that temptation with a shake of his head. No point in being stupid.

But something is different. He feels it, first on the bus, then on his walk, during his cigarette break before work and even as he enters the brightly lit eatery, he still senses something is wrong.

There's a sparkly look to everything that strikes him as un-usual and rather than address the cook, he keeps his head down and gets to the first batch of dishes in the sink. He doesn't know if he's dreaming or not.

His day goes on and he's just about feeling normal when he notices a customer standing by the counter through the hole in the wall that the cook generally pushes plates through when the waitress is working. The figure is short and heavily dressed for the weather. He's got a baseball hat hiding chin-length hair and a walkie talkie on his belt. He wears jeans and a flannel jacket over another layer of clothing. Too hot for this weather, thinks Tommy again.

The walkie talkie comes to life.

"We're just living' life in freedom now, there's something in the air." The speaker crackles. Tommy finds himself entranced, the voice is high and melodic, but still displays some California twang.

"If you want to know about this country, just look out the window." The voice continues. The customer abruptly hits a button and quickly sprints out of the diner. Tommy can't help himself, he stands motionless for a second, then suddenly runs to the door. The cook yells something as he brushes past him, but

Tommy doesn't care.

He has to hear that voice. Meet this man. He needs that feeling of bliss and empathy that he used to visualize so clearly before he'd made his way to this Coast, when he slept in alleyways and begged on the street and sold his first sack of cocaine and shot up his first dose of heroin…

But there's no one outside, not even a breeze. There's nowhere the figure could've gotten away to so quickly and Tommy stands in the open door with a slack jawed expression. The cook yells something again and Suzy is looking at him with disappointment in her eyes. Tommy knows he's in for it, but he reluctantly closes the door and gets back to work.

"Don't know what you were running for," the cook says as Tommy muscles his way back to the sink. "Place has been dead all day. What, you really need a break? Thought you saw a movie star, or something?"

Tommy mumbles an apology and fills a pan with water. At the end of the shift, Suzy announces he's on vacation for the next week. He takes the proffered money, his pay for the day, picks up his pack, still stunned, and walks to the subway to get a connection bus route to pick up for the weekend. He knew he could never stop being a scumbag.

*   *   *

But Zeke is not on the pier. It's really quite astounding, a junkie is very rarely late and lately Zeke has fallen from his lofty perch as a dealer and has become a user again. The signs of his demise had always been in the making, Tommy considers, but they'd been subtle for a long time. Now was just the advent of a heroin laced summer. Tommy doesn't mind. He is getting out of the game, he thinks, ignoring the day behind him and the long week ahead of sitting in the park selling the drugs that Zeke was supposed to have, but couldn't be bothered to be on time for.

He waits for an hour, maybe two, strolling along the beach when he doesn't feel like standing on the pier. He uses the bathroom, buys some fried food and generally hangs. He listens to the first musicians of the season. There was some new rhumba band. He sits at the edge of the massive pier. They're pretty good. Tommy leaves a few dollars in their jar.

Eventually, though, he realizes that he's outstayed his welcome and his purpose was becoming obvious. That was just the way of it. Without plans, he thinks, everyone is aware of your number.

So, he makes the trek to Zeke's house. Confront the geek directly or screw his girlfriend. Fuck all this, he thinks, I'm getting out. The call of the easy money has kept him going for too long now and he's getting out, just a few more handouts, then, then… then what? It's an irritable boy that arrives at the drug house, but he isn't really aware that dark is falling and his time is running out.

Zeke isn't at the house either, but the lights are on and Tommy slams open the door. Mike and Sisi both look up. Mike on the couch. Sisi doing her toenails on the recliner. Neither say anything.

Mike lurches his skinny frame from on the couch and pulls out a shopping bag. Tommy grabs it and then turns away.

"Don't be a stranger," says Sisi. Tommy walks out and makes his way back to Hollywood. His eyes are full of tears.

5.

The scene of Hollywood on a weekend can get pretty crazy. The tourist attractions, the huge malls, all the day time traffic shifts when night falls. Soon, large crowds of people start gallivanting for their night out. Tight dresses, impeccably kept night gear is on the order for the festivities. Normal, everyday people become the predators and the victims of a society that let's nothing past it and stops for no one. Tommy had made his way into these crowds many times before, late after long days of begging on the sidewalk, also transformed by the occult-like ceremony of the town. It is almost a new millennium and no one knows it more that the shakers and dealers of these hills.

Smoking a cigarette, Tommy stashes the drugs into his pack and looks like a worker hurrying to his job. The crowd doesn't so much as dissipate around him as he wedges himself from small cranny to tight nook until he's at the front of the line. The guy at the door doesn't look happy and gives Tommy a disgusted look as he lugs his way past. Very unprofessional on his part, thinks Tommy.

Inside, the place is bristling. Tommy finds himself in a circle of young men, all decked out in punk fashion, Ramones era. They speak in short intervals, drinking sips of beer. On stage, a band is setting up under heavy bright lights and Tommy tries to visualize himself stepping up to that height and cornering his way to the back stage through them, but then spots the big guy looking around by the hallway to the door.

The door. It feels suddenly very claustrophobic for Tommy. The forbidden decadence of the club creeps into his bones and he suddenly feels very afraid and humbled by the scene. What is he doing here?

He stumbles to his boss and is directed to the back room through another door. His suit is on the dressing table and a bottle of scotch. Compliments for the band, thinks Tommy, taking a moment to unscrew the bottle and take a deep gulp. His lungs on fire, he pulls a smoke from his discarded pants still sweaty from travel and work. For a few minutes, he thinks of nothing and just loses a part of himself to the night.

In the small passageway between in and out, Tommy nurses his bat, sometimes putting on his ski mask, quietly humming. Business is bustling. The big guy walks in almost every other quarter hour. Money is piling up. At the end of the night, Tommy would take his cut which was largely whatever the big man had in his pocket, along with the excess drugs that he could feed to his daytime custies. Feels almost Mafioso, but what other choice does he have? Tommy curses himself every time the door closes. It's like being a rat in a cage.

Then it happens. Tommy hears the knock almost subconsciously and fear hits him. What the fuck? What was he going to do? He hears the big man say something about outside, the footsteps leading away.

He pulls the ski-mask on, opens the outer door, then walks out it. His hands are sweaty and his breathing is fast. He steps right outside the wall, hiding the bat behind his body and waits. It seems he waits for a long time.

All of a sudden, figures come off the street. He hears the big man saying something and sees two youths following him in tight jeans and leather jackets, medium cut hair fluttering in an unnatural breeze. The big man stops, a few yards from him.

"Ok, boys," he says. "Here's the guy."

"Right," Tommy whispers.

Breathing deeply, he smashes the first teenager in the shoulder as he's reaching out with some twenties. Then the kid was on the ground and Tommy hits him in the side with the point of the bat, then turns to the other who's looking at his fallen friend.

"Get out," he growls and holds up the bat. The youth grabs his friend by the arm and the two of them back out. It's too dark to see clearly, but Tommy is in another space anyway. Like a video game. He menacingly shakes the bat while the big man chuckles beside him. The boys get to the corner and are gone.

"Good job, kid," says the big man. Tommy nods. Nothing else happens that night.

*   *   *

Back at Stephanie's, Tommy is feeling good. Stephanie is in the shower and she's been in there for some time. He wonders if she's doing dope without him! He doesn't care. While he'd always technically been a felon and before that a rebel, he'd never had to get physical before. It was another phase in the story of a hardened criminal. It was easy to consider oneself a business man with the goods and services and all, but sometimes things got real. Tommy decides not to think about it and lies heavily on the bed, a kink in the right side of his soul making his ribs hurt. If there was any retribution in the next life, Tommy felt sure it'd be a kick in the head.

Almost too precisely, Stephanie comes in and starts talking about Buddhism and reincarnation and Hare Krishna. She's saying it's really interesting and maybe those guys in the 60's had something, but for Tommy, it's all a drone. What if he becomes a beaten dog in his next life and how soon was that from now? He supposes the two victims were just kids, but what if they came back? All these little deals pile up in his mind.

"It's like life, real life, is always in ascension around the universe," she says. "And we're making the choices of what's moral, what's experience. We're filling in the palette of god!"

Tommy smiles and closes his eyes. There's not a lot more to say. He feels satisfied, there's no work today and there's no more drugs to pawn off. The big guy had cleaned him out of all of them that night and had paid quite handsomely. Stephanie wants to go to the zoo and Tommy doesn't care at all.

*　　*　　*

A few days later he's whistling on the beach and taking the time to enjoy himself. He's really nothing, just a cog in a machine, but he's at peace. He walks the entire beach twice, then thinks about going over to Zeke's for a quick look around. He's a little worried this money and drug train ala Zeke will falter, slow and stop just as he's making headway in the game. Christ, what if he was forced just to rely on his salary at the diner and coins off the street? Hadn't he just been thinking how great it would be to go legit and get out?

He blocks the thought and mentally gets himself suited for the day. While he can still just make some excuse to the big man, lack of supplies or some reason like that, he knows eventually he'll be broke. So, he might as well get over it now and head to his dealer's house. He doesn't know what kind of mood Zeke'll be in and sad as it was, his continued support was like a leg on a chair. Tommy depended on Zeke's goodwill.

And her's. Sisi was still the unattainable angel in his thoughts. Tommy guesses that he just felt Stephanie was too young and cramped his style. Maybe it was simply that Stephanie was a drug addict while Sisi hardly even took a drink. Strength. Discipline. Clarity. That's what was attractive in his eyes.

Not that he and Stephanie didn't have a lot in common. They were both punk rockers who wanted out of the system, the city, the machine. Already, Tommy knew he'd regret his own desires and be back at Stephanie's, working out their relationship, but damned if he wasn't sick of the whole thing.

He is sick of all the words tumbling their way out of his mouth, he thinks. Sisi, though, she'd just make it her and him, just soul energy with flashes of genuine glee. Tommy waits for the contradictory monogamous piece of his brain to pipe up, but it just grumbled. That's what it used to be with Stephanie, it says finally. Tommy agrees. He wants it again and that's why he decides to go to his dealer's home. Maybe he could work something out that made her see he was better than Zeke or Mike or anyone.

He stops though, his attention suddenly taken by a couple kids walking in his direction. They're just walking, taking full strides without smiling. One is wearing sun-glasses and he suddenly hits the other in the shoulder. They both are looking at him and one calls out.

"Rob?"

Tommy stares at them incredulously. His heart beats in his chest as they run towards him. They are instantly recognizable as his friends from home, Andy and Tony. A thousand miles away to two feet. It was nuts.

"Rob? Rob! What are you doing here?" asks Andy.

"Whatever he's doing here, he's doing it with us," says Tony.

Tommy smiles, half-unconsciously.

"What do you say?" Tony continues.

"What are you doing here, man? Where are you staying?" asks Andy.

"I've got a girl." The words come out of Tommy's mouth like glue from a tube. "I'm doing well, actually, really."

"Well, we're in town looking at colleges. Would you like to come?"

"No, no," says Tommy, very uncertain. "I've got to go... bye?" He turns to leave. What's going on?

"Wait a minute, you're not going to just leave us, I mean, here we are... we're not going to tell anybody... force you home..."

"It's not like that," says Tommy, still a bit monosyllabic. His

stomach is starting to ache and there's no way out of this unbe-
lievable situation. "I plan to go home. Soon. Not now." He tries to
turn again. How in the hell?

"Well, at least meet us tomorrow? Right here, 10 o'clock.
We're flying back in two days. Man, we've been through some
times. Couple nights ago we almost got the shit kicked out of us
by this guy with a bat. Oh, man, it was so crazy!"

Slowly, the wheels in Tommy's mind turn and he realizes with
a start that Tony was favoring his shoulder. Click, click, click. The
urge to leave had been a stream, but now the nuclear power plant
was exploding leaving radioactive waste across the valley in a
plume of green water.

"I gotta go," he says. "Yeah, I'll meet you tomorrow."

The two ex-friends stand helplessly, thinking how frail their
boyhood pal appears.

"Gina misses you," says Andy softly.

"I know," says Tommy. "But I really gotta go." He forces a
smile. "Tomorrow, ok?"

"Ok." The three stand awkwardly, then slowly turn in opposite directions. Tommy starts off at a quick walking pace. He
needs to go home, but where is that? Stephanie is at school and
he's fired from the diner for now... he realizes suddenly that he's
already made up his mind.

*   *   *

He gets to the house and runs up the walkway, pushes into
the door and immediately sees Zeke laying on the couch.

"Hey!" he says, getting up.

"Where's Sisi?" ask Tommy, out of breath.

"What? Oh, she's gone shopping… wait, did she short you the other night? I'm gonna kill that bitch!" He trails off, then looks at the floor.

"Do you have the money for that? I won't hold it against you, fuck women… but I could use it." Zeke looks like he's in a bad way, almost dangerously so. Tommy's eyes go to the ripped pillow and fluff just strewn around the room. He had walked into a battle zone.

"It's not that," he says before thinking. "I… I just wanted to ask her about something." He finishes lamely.

"Oh, ok, but about that money…" Tommy grabs the cash from his wallet and hands it carefully to Zeke. The tension drains from Zeke's features and he actually smiles.

"So," he says. "Want a shot?"

And Tommy realizes that was all he was looking for. All the gears and anxieties seemed to slow down and stop as he recognizes this permanent solution. Who needed Sisi when you had heroin?

6.

Zeke and Tommy speak to each other in slurred, drugged up ways. The light from the windows streams across the room, mirroring the feeling rushing through each of them. They're comrades, brothers, friends. The time slips by and at some point Sisi comes home with Mike toting grocery bags, but the two of them, Zeke and Tommy, just smile and close their eyes as they recline on the couch and bean-bag. It's a good life. It's fuckin' amazing and Tommy feels the sense of peace he's been looking for. So long now. Why had he run?

He wonders to himself. Careless, he thinks. He'd forgotten the best things in life. Tomorrow he'll curse himself for giving in, but now he was blessed and stoked and indescribably happy. Stephanie could wait. His job could wait, His family, everyone. All the thoughts of moving beyond this were nonexistent.

"I think I should go," he says, half-sleeping. Zeke nods and pulls his head back to his shoulders.

"Yeah, ok, see you soon…"

"Ok," Tommy doesn't know why he's leaving. His stomach is turning not at all unpleasant. He stands.

"I think I need to use your bathroom," he slurs. He stumbles to the far wall. In the next room, he hears the wet sounds of sex. He completes his journey to the toilet and vomits. It feels lovely.

Wiping the bile off his face, he gets to the living room, then his figure is framed in the bright doorway.

"Bye, Zeke," he says. "Thanks."

*   *   *

"Ok, Tommy," says Sisi, sitting on the bus with Tommy's half passed out body. "I needed someone and you're so young. I never meant to hurt you. Especially not you. It's not something that was planned." In the corner of the bus, Kurt plays left-handed guitar and the bus stops periodically. He knows he's hallucinating, but it's impossible to stop. Just go with it.

"Don't worry," he says, tries to say. "I hope you guys are happy." Mike walks up to Kurt, shouts and waves his hands around. "The two of you can make it."

"Y'know, we started with pills, but Mike turned me... I turned to heroin, y'know? It is very good. Zeke never let me have any." She finishes with a glum look. "I'm sorry Tommy."

"It's ok." The bus stops.

"Last stop," calls the driver.

Tommy lurches off his seat and exits the bus into some evening neighborhood. He's all alone.

*   *   *

Things can get pretty fucked up on the streets. Tommy couldn't even count the amount of mishaps, fights and disagreements between the homeless and the housed and even the dealers in the park would get rowdy. Sometimes he'd find himself in a little community of squatters and have to leave straight up in the morning before the cops came to kick them out. Arguments, mix-ups, missing persons, even loud make-up sex. These scenes were not unfamiliar to his eyes. As he'd said, he isn't close to the other homeless. He doesn't get into relationships, hitch hike to San Fran, get drunk and stupid with just anybody, but he was considered a cool dude. Certainly not the enemy.

If they know him at all, which many did not with newcomers making the scene daily and weekly, they'd probably say he was nice, but quiet. That's what he was passionate about, just staying out of the fray. But tonight was not one of those nights.

Carefully, he makes his way back to the Sunset Strip. It's hard work. He had to memorize bus schedules, get change for the ride, stay awake to actually get on the bus and then not act too weird for the average public transportation customer. At one point an obviously deranged man gets on and finds his way next to Tommy.

"Man, man!" he says, fidgeting with his hands. "You on something? I'm talking to you, man, man, man." Tommy just stares out the window. Eventually the man leaves him to go back into whatever primordial soup he'd come from. Too many crazies in the street. He guesses that it's the result of Reaganomics, recalling a conversation with another man months ago. The guy had actually given him a card to a local school. He was a professor.

But he gets there, god knows how, but he gets there. It isn't a friendly reception. He thinks about going to the diner, his day job was still open for all he knows, but he pukes on the sidewalk and that's the end of that thought train. Gotta get somewhere, gotta be somewhere.

He walks to the bridge and some slight, blonde haired girl

is sleeping on the mattress. He doesn't even care. He swings his body next to her and closes his eyes. The girl just lies there moaning, on some drug or another. Pretty soon he's getting bleary eyed, whether from drugs or newfound sickness. Can't be sure, but he lays there all night and in the morning, gets up to go see his real friends, from before all this, on the sunny beach of the Pacific Sea.

He gets to the beach, sun already high in the sky, looks around at the milling people. He tries to skip a little, shake his hair free of any dirt or possible vomit. There didn't seem to be any of that, but Tommy shakes it anyway. The air is warm, getting warmer as he steadily makes his way to the predetermined spot. He gets there and looks around. There are no familiar faces in the crowd, so he leans on his knees, stretches and waits.

What had it all been worth? Every event in his life seemed to be from a cheap movie. He certainly hadn't learned anything from it. As he tries to relax he feels a tension come through his chest. His pack seems overwhelmingly heavy. He takes it off, then moves to the sand and sits on it heavily. He feels really sick.

Just then he hears a voice and for a second he assumes it's a hallucination, but it doesn't continue on like the voices he normally hears. The voices in your head know you're listening and don't care if you ignore them.

"Hey man?" the voice turns out to be one of the two beggars he met downtown. Why the hell are they bothering him? Is he a public servant or something?

"Hey," he replies. He looks for their yuppie components, his two idiot friends from Massachusetts. Sure enough, they show up on cue.

"Hey, Rob," says Tony smiling, clean, sparkly really.

"Hey, man," says Andy. So, the four of them stand around Tommy, the hero of this discordant tale. There seems to be a moment of confrontation, a tension in the air, or at least that's what Tommy perceives. However, Tommy is now feeling the pangs of nausea, an effect of heroin withdrawal.

"I gotta go," he suddenly says. His friends look perplexed. Gus and Matt appear to be paying attention to the ocean. Scratching his belly, Gus taps his foot to some silent music.

"Hey," says Andy again, but this time to the unexplained duo. "I'm Andy, do you guys know Rob here?"

"A bit here, bit there," says Matt. "We're street kids. Just traveled from Oregon."

"Are you a traveler too, Rob?" asks Tony.

Tommy tries to shake his head. His vision is spinning. He guesses his first statement had been too quiet to hear. He says it again.

"I gotta go."

"Why the hurry?" Matt asks. "We're just conversing. Hey, we aren't tripping you out are we? Are you on acid or something?"

Tommy's world is revolving unsteadily. It's just then that he sees a black and white figure sprinting towards him. He knows who it is immediately. It's his former friend. A bad mess of drugs and violence. Zeke was coming for him.

There isn't a moment of hesitation. Tommy doesn't even think. He knows he is a dead man. He rises to his feet, never minding the pack and starts running away. The four kids around him watch him go, perplexed and are then scattered as Zeke's busts through their little group.

"Whoa," says Tony.

"Yeah, things can get kinda weird," replies Gus. He smiles before squinting into the space Tommy and Zeke had just exited. Immediately, he jumps into a run following the pair. The others follow.

Tommy is too far away at this point, just dashing towards the pier. He needs to get around people, he's thinking, that's the only way to safety. Just then he feels his body tense up just as his foot hits the pier and he is propelled into a bad dive towards the ground. He feels a hand grab his shirt, then his arm. Zeke is on him, straddling his chest with murder in his eyes.

"You took her!" he screams. "You took me! You're a filthy rat and I'm going to kill you!"

Tommy tries to struggle, but it's useless. His friends are too far away, he doesn't know why he'd run from their protection and the junkie is just too strong as he pulls something out of the back of his belt. Tommy realizes with sickening certainty that it's a gun. He wishes, all of a sudden, for a quick and painless death, but he's screaming for help, for anybody or anything to save him.

"I loved her!" screams Zeke. "And you and that bozo took turns with her every night! Didn't you! You fucked her and you fucked me! I'm not going to stand for it! I'm not going to be your bitch…!"

Some bodybuilder grabs him with both arms and Tommy is free! He gets up and runs down the beach again.

"See you!" he yells as he passes his friends who hadn't even the chance to react and runs, runs, toward the city. The police never found him. He was on a rooftop. Huddling low to avoid detection. He was done. He was going to Stephanie's and they were getting the hell out of there. They were going somewhere new; he was continuing his flight.

When he gets to Stephanie's he is still rabid from fear. She answers the door in her kind, dazed way and takes him in. He can barely talk. Stephanie thinks he's tripping and helps him undress and puts him to bed. He sleeps the rest of the day.

"Quiet now little one," she says calmly and out of pure exhaustion and adrenaline, Tommy doesn't feel sick, he just passes out like a bad dream. Too much excitement, thinks Stephanie and goes into the living room to continue her shows. The television is shining and she half watches for the rest of the night. It is April 5th, 1994.

*   *   *

Tommy has spent all this time looking for that feeling that would keep going like an endless note played on electric guitar. Like Nirvana. A state of abject happiness and enlightenment. But now he knows that it's impossible. There would always be commitments, layers of society he would never agree with. There'd be work and school and family and love. The thought of it, of all the suffering made him toss in his sleep.

But bygone, he was going to do it this time! He was going to go back to that dishwashing job. He was going to call those yuppies at the bar. He was going to make plans for him and Stephanie and once summer hits he'll learn how to surf, how to skate, how to shoot movies and act and he'd get off the drugs…

He moans a little at the thought. Clean and stable. He'd call his mother and father and sister and make everything right... Maybe he'd even go back to school… friends, family, love and career…

He thinks all of this inside his head, but a cold sweat breaks out. He wonders… Haven't we heard this all before? Tommy, there's going to be work and more work. Hard labor, talks about relationships, boredom. That sad, sad grey feeling not knowing who he is or where he belongs… what can be said?

He has to position himself for all of these.

But there'll be a time to have that feeling, too, he thinks as he rolls over in bed. There'd be time for Nirvana, for enlightenment and oneness with everything. His body would fail, but his soul would continue. Somewhere in his fever-movements, he finds a momentary peace.

It was all to the beating of a bass drum and almost violent grinding of guitars and bass. He'd get there, he'd see… But it isn't attained by an endless, frantic race of loss and depleting youth. Like heroin. Like loneliness. He knows that now.

There are no waves of peace stalking on the shore that he'll never achieve. He's being shown the way. Today Kurt Cobain died. Long live the king. The king is dead, but long live the king.

Acknowledgements

This book was not made in a vacuum. Firstly I'd like to thank Erik Radvon for holding onto the original manuscript that became the first 50 pages of this novel. He has also been a constant support in writing and life.

Dylan Harris took a lot of time to read, grammatically correct my sentences, and even help out with flow of each paragraph. She certainly has a career of editing and I'm honored that she took the time to edit this.

Philip Burke is responsible for the stunning cover-art of this book. He and his family have been supportive and dedicated to ensuring that I'm protected as I continue to write and evolve by introducing me to Buddhism.

I'd also like to thank Justin Karcher and the rest of Ghost City Press, as well as Amy Kinsman at Riggwelter for agreeing to publish excerpts of "Nirvana Dreams" for their audiences.

Finally I'd like to thank Mike Santillo for putting me in contact with No Frills Buffalo and Mark Pogodzinski. Mark has been incredibly patient with me and very accepting of delays and changes with this manuscript.

About the Author

Benjamin Joe lives in Buffalo, New York where he works as a freelance writer for The Niagara Gazette and IP-Watchdog.org. When he's not making a deadline, he's honing his craft regarding short stories and full-length novels.